The Education of Bet

BY LAUREN BARATZ-LOGSTED

Houghton Mifflin Harcourt
Boston New York 2010

For Jack Baratz (1921–1992),
my father, a man who believed
in stretching the mind every day:
I still miss you, Dad.

Houghton Mifflin is an imprint of
Houghton Mifflin Harcourt Publishing Company.

www.hmhbooks.com

The text of this book is set in Adobe Garamond.
Book design by Susanna Vagt.

Library of Congress Cataloging-in-Publication Data
Baratz-Logsted, Lauren.
The education of Bet / by Lauren Baratz-Logsted.
p. cm.
Summary: Denied an education because of both her gender and background, sixteen-year-old Elizabeth cuts her hair and alters suits belonging to Will, her wealthy patron's grandnephew, to take his place at school while Will pursues a military career in nineteenth-century England.
ISBN 978-0-547-22308-7
[1. Sex role—Fiction. 2. Schools—Fiction. 3. Social classes—Fiction. 4. Orphans—Fiction. 5. Great Britain—History—19th century—Fiction.] I. Title.
PZ7.B22966Edu 2010
[Fic]—dc22 2009049710

Manufactured in the United States of America
DOC 10 9 8 7 6 5 4 3 2 1

4500225990

Thanks go to:
Julia Richardson, for being my kind of editor;
Pamela Harty, for being my kind of agent;
Lauren Catherine, Greg Logsted, Robert Mayette, and
Andrea Schicke Hirsh, for being my kind of writing group partners;
Lucille Baratz, for being my kind of mother;
Greg Logsted, for being my kind of husband;
Jackie Logsted, for being my kind of daughter.
As you can see, my world is filled with my kind of people.
I am a very lucky woman, indeed.

prologue

Everything I needed to wear beneath my clothes was already in place.

I selected a shirt the color of unspoiled snow, eased my arms into the sleeves, slowly did up the buttons from narrow waist to chest and finally to neck. It felt peculiar to wear something on my upper body, in particular my waist, that did not bind my skin like a glove. How odd not to feel constricted where one expected to. The trousers that I slid up over the slight swell of my hips were made of black superfine wool, and I buttoned these as well. This was even more peculiar, the sensation of the expensive fabric against my calves and thighs.

A sound in the outer hallway brought me up short. Was someone coming? The threat of intrusion, of discovery before I'd finished, terrified me. It was a danger I lived with daily, as natural to my new life as a lack of danger had been to my old one. But after a long moment spent stock-still, hearing no more noises, I concluded that the sounds were of my imagination's making, a product of my fears.

I was well practiced in the art of tying ties, and I commenced doing so now, taking up the length of black silk and fitting it around my collar. Then I took the ends and fashioned a knot that I knew without looking would fall at a slightly rakish angle. My intention was to convey that perfect mix of convention (I was wearing a tie) and indifference to convention (I did not care how that tie looked). Over all, I put on a black superfine wool coat that matched the trousers.

Only then, when I was fully dressed except for shoes, did I turn to confront my reflection in the looking glass.

And what did I see there?

A clean-shaven young gentleman about sixteen years of age, with thick black hair so wavy there was almost a curl to it—there would be, on humid days—and eyes nearly as dark; pale skin; generous lips; a fine straight nose. The young man looking back at me was handsome and gave off an air of self-confidence.

There was just one problem; two, actually.

The barely discernible bulge in the front of the trousers had been created by a carefully balled-up pair of stockings.

And the young gentleman—*I*—was a girl.

CHAPTER *one*

"William, I am *so* disappointed in you!"

Paul Gardener always addressed his great-nephew as William when he was displeased with something he had done.

I was seated on a chair by the fireplace, sewing, my long skirts around me, as I had been just a moment before when a servant at the door to the drawing room had announced Will. The drawing room ran the length of the house, from front to back, and had large windows at either end that cast long shadows now that night was nearly upon us. The ceiling was a blinding white, while the walls were painted scarlet, punctuated with well-placed brass candle fixtures; the master of the house and I were seated at the room's far end. There was an enormous area rug, also in scarlet but accented with cream, and a large bookcase containing all of the master's favorite volumes, of which I'd read more than a few.

"Bet." Will acknowledged me with a nod after first greeting his great-uncle, as was proper.

"Will." I returned the nod but saw no reason to rise for the occasion, although I was happy to see him. I was always happy to see Will, no matter what the circumstances.

Paul Gardener did not rise either. It was difficult for him to do so without assistance. In the past few years, he had aged a great deal. Indeed, both eyes, formerly a sharp blue, were now so fogged by cataracts that he glimpsed only flashes of the world through thick clouds, and it was one of my jobs to read to him from the papers or from books when he was of a mind to be read to. Still, despite his many infirmities, Paul Gardener took great care in his dress and appearance; his proud mane of hair was white and thick. I had seen artists' renderings of him when he was younger and knew that in his youth he had been nearly as handsome as Will.

"I had somewhat hoped you would be happy to see me, Uncle," Will said with a wry smile.

I dared look at Will no longer for fear I would break out into laughter, so I cast my gaze back down upon my sewing. It was not so much that the sewing needed to be done as that I needed something to do.

"Of *course* I am happy to see you!" the old man sputtered. He looked befuddled for a moment as he corrected himself, "Well, that is, if I *could* see you." After that brief moment of befuddlement, he recalled his outrage. Raising a gnarled fist, he shook the sheet of paper he held clenched in his hand. It was a letter, and ever since I'd read its contents to him last week, he'd been holding it pretty much every moment I had seen him. "What," he thundered, "is the meaning of this?"

Without needing to look at what his great-uncle was holding, Will knew to what he was referring.

"It means," he said, "that I have been sent down from school."

Which is a nice way, I thought, *of saying that you have been expelled.*

"I understand that!" the old man said. "I may be blind, or near enough, but I am not stupid. But what I don't understand—what I cannot understand, William—is *why?*"

Will's expression softened from its usual air of studied indifference. Whatever else Will was, he did not like to hurt his great-uncle; still, he would not do what was against his nature merely to please. He opened his mouth to speak—perhaps even to make an effort to sound contrite—but he was stopped by the grandfather clock at the other end of the room banging out the hour.

"Oh." Paul Gardener lowered his fist. "It is time for dinner."

No matter what was going on around him—including storms outside or within the house—Paul Gardener would have his meals on time.

"The Boers could show up here in London," Will had said to me on his last visit home, "they could march up right to our door and enter, weapons drawn, and Uncle would say, 'You may kill me in half an hour, but first I must finish my supper.'"

Will approached his great-uncle's chair and, placing his strong hand under the elderly man's elbow, helped him to his feet. "Uncle?" Will invited, holding his own elbow out so that he might escort the old man to the dining room.

They were nearly through the doorway when Paul Gardener paused and cocked his head, listening. His eyesight may have been awful, but his hearing was perfect.

"Elizabeth?" he called back to me, having detected the absence of any following footsteps. "Aren't you dining with us this evening?"

He said this as though I were always welcome at the table, and yet I always waited to be asked, never assuming anything. I knew that indeed my presence was *not* always welcome.

"Of course, sir," I said, at once setting aside my sewing. It would never have occurred to me to say no.

As I followed behind them, I saw Will turn his head and glance back at me over his great-uncle's shoulder. His smile was devilish, and I returned it in full.

You, Will, I thought, *have just been saved by the bell.*

But that saving did not last long, not even through the soup course.

"Really, William, how many times does this make that you have been sent down from a school? Is this the second or the third?"

The dining room was another long room—really, the entire house was filled with long things—and the walls were covered in white wallpaper with a rose pattern. There were framed mirrors on three walls, a china closet, a curio cabinet, and a sideboard on which breakfast was often set out. A large Oriental carpet covered much of the hardwood floor, and the chairs we sat on were ornate, the seats and backs covered in rose crushed velvet, the carved mahogany trim intricate. The mahogany table itself could have sat twenty easily, but we three congregated at one end, Paul Gardener at the head while Will and I faced each other.

Overhead, the chandelier shimmered brilliantly.

"It is the fourth," Will admitted, at least having the grace to look embarrassed at this admission.

"The *fourth!*"

A maid entered, Molly, and she silently proceeded to bring the platter of roast beef to the master. Sara followed behind her with the potatoes, and Ann brought up the rear with the assorted vegetables.

"This last does not really count as being *sent down,*" Will said, smiling as though pleased to be able to make this distinction.

The old man looked surprised. "It doesn't?"

"Not at all," Will said as Molly brought the platter to his side. "Since it was end of term, and we were all going home anyway, this falls more under the heading of my being requested never to return."

"Oh." The old man looked as though his great-nephew had succeeded in scoring an important point. "I see."

Sometimes I wondered if there was anything Will couldn't get away with.

Will studied the food on his plate, and I took advantage of his being preoccupied to look at him.

Will and I had much in common in terms of appearance. Really, given how alike we were, it was no wonder I sometimes thought of Will as my brother. I was very tall for a girl, and we were both lean, although I had some slight curves in places he did not. We both had dark eyes—although his proud eyebrows were slightly heavier, and my lashes were longer—and black hair. The texture of our hair was even similar: wavy with a tendency to curl when the weather was humid. Of course, my hair was very long while his was trimmed much shorter. Oh, and I did not need to shave.

Funny, I did not think myself pretty, and yet I did find Will handsome.

"Miss Smith?"

Those two words called my attention back, and looking to my side, I saw Molly standing there, waiting for me to serve myself from the platter.

The servants always called me Miss Smith whenever the master and Will were around, but simply Elizabeth when they were not. It was a thing I had never gotten used to, as though I were two different people in one body.

"Thank you, Molly," I said, helping myself.

She dipped a curtsy, as she had done after serving the other two, but the one she dipped for me seemed to have some irony to it.

Well, who could blame her?

"Elizabeth?" The old man turned to me once all the servants had left. "Can you remember all the reasons William has been sent down from school or, er, requested never to return?"

I wondered if he really could have forgotten them. I did not like being put in a position where I had to say anything negative about anyone else in the household—my own place felt far too tenuous—but I could not simply ignore a direct question. Well, perhaps if Will were the one asking.

"Let me see . . ." I tilted my head toward the ceiling as though it would take a great effort to remember, as though Will's scholastic crimes weren't so notable that of course they sprang readily to mind.

"The first time was cheating," I said, then stopped myself. "No, that's not right. Will had to build up to that. The first time was lying, it was the *second* time that was cheating, the third time was general mischief—too many fights and that sort of thing—while this last time, the fourth time—"

I had to stop myself again, truly puzzled. "Why, I don't know what the fourth time was. The letter never said."

His great-uncle and I both turned in Will's direction, questioning looks on our faces.

"I, um, set the headmaster's house on fire," Will said.

The old man practically jumped out of his seat. "You set—?"

"But there was no one inside it at the time," Will quickly added.

"You set—? You could have been arrested! You *should* have been arrested! Why weren't—"

"It was a decrepit house," Will said. "The headmaster needed a new one." Then he laughed. "Really, I think he was rather grateful for my efforts, but of course he couldn't say *that,* so I was merely asked never to return."

"You're an arsonist!"

Will shrugged. "Not if I was never charged with any crime."

Although I'd often thought that Will could probably get away with anything, I did marvel at times that schools kept accepting him, given his history. But then, all I needed to do was look around me, taking in the evidence of the enormous wealth of Paul Gardener and the power I knew went with it. As long as Will had a great-uncle who could buy him out of trouble, schools would continue to accept him; the ones that had been provoked into expelling him had done so only with great reluctance and much apologizing. Were it not for his great-uncle's money and influence, Will would no doubt have become a social pariah for his misdeeds, been kept away from the best of society.

"I don't understand." The old man threw down his napkin in despair. "You have had every advantage. And you are smart! Why must you lie? Why must you cheat? Why must you do all of these awful . . . *things?*"

For once, Will, who always had an answer for everything, remained silent.

If his great-uncle had asked me, I could have answered that question. But he hadn't, and I was glad of that. Will did not like to hurt his great-uncle, and I did not like to do so either; I would never even consider it unless something truly important was at stake.

"It is almost," the old man said, as though he had seized upon a shrewd thought, "as though you do not *want* to be at school."

I almost laughed out loud at this, and from the look on his face, Will was having a similar reaction.

"But it does not matter what you want," the old man went on, steely now, no longer bothering to wonder why Will did the things he did. "By the end of summer I will have found you yet another school, no matter who I have to bribe or how much it costs me. I don't even care if it is the worst school in all of England—which is probably the only sort of place that would accept you at this point—this time, *you will not get sent down!*"

We went back in the drawing room, where Paul Gardener asked for the pudding course to be served, following which he poured a glass of port and requested that I read to him.

Will made to leave, but, having heard the sound of retreating footsteps, his great-uncle called him back.

"You will listen to Elizabeth read," the old man commanded. "Who knows? You might even learn something."

So Will slouched in a chair, hands clasped behind his head, long legs stretched out in front of him, looking bored out of his mind as I read from *King Lear.*

The old man liked me to read Shakespeare to him, liked that I had a talent for creating different voices for all the characters so he never had to ask me who was speaking, but not many pages in he was snoring in his seat.

"Come outside with me, Bet?" Will invited.

I placed a piece of red silk ribbon to mark the spot where I'd left off reading and gently put the volume aside. Then I followed Will out of the room, to the rear of the house, and through the French doors that led to the back garden.

Taking a seat on the curved stone bench, I watched as Will paced under the early moonlight.

With no more sun, and with summer proper yet to get under way, it was chilly out. Could we not, I wondered as I rubbed my hands over my arms for warmth, have discussed whatever Will wanted to discuss inside?

"If I have to go back to that school, I will go *mad!*" Will erupted.

"Well," I said, reasonably enough, "you do not have to go back to that school. In fact, you *cannot* go back to that school."

"Any school, then," he said, seething.

"Will you please stop pacing?" I said. "It is dizzy-making watching you go back and forth like this."

"Fine." Will still seethed but at least he obeyed my request, coming to sit beside me.

"Your great-uncle is right," I said. "Your behavior makes no sense. You are smart enough to do well in school, very well, and yet you choose not to. You are good enough not to do the awful things you do, and yet you choose to do them anyway."

"Yes, yes, I am a puzzle to everybody. Please, Bet," he said. "You're not going to say 'Why, Will?' to me too, are you?"

"No, of course not. I know why you do as you do. It is because you do not wish to be where you are."

"Yes!" His sense of relief at being understood for once was so strong I could almost reach out and touch it with my hand, touch him to show my sympathy.

And yet I couldn't do that. It was rare for me to touch another person and just as rare to have another person touch me.

So instead I settled for unleashing my anger. Will and I had known each other long enough that I could do that in front of him, provided we were alone; I could do it in front of no one else in the world.

"And do *you* have any idea," I said, "how *insanely* angry you make me?"

He drew back at this, startled.

I continued before he could stop me.

"I can read just as well as you can, Will Gardener! I am just as smart as you are! And yet I am stuck here, in this house, while you"—now it was my turn to seethe, and I gestured toward him with my hand, disgusted—"you are out there in the world!"

"You are right," he admitted softly. "It is not fair."

That softness, that sensitivity, was almost harder to bear than his infuriating behavior. In a way, I felt as though he'd be doing me a favor if he were to laugh at my ambition. Perhaps if he did, I would think my desires silly as well, and eventually, one day, I would stop wanting what I could not have.

"Right," I said, crossing my arms firmly against my chest. "It is not fair."

"But it is the way of the world," he said.

I did not like this so much. I did not like thinking anything impossible. But now I worried that if we continued on in this vein, I would burst into tears of frustration in front of him, and this I did not want to do.

So I changed the subject.

"Tell me, Will. I know you do not want to be at school—I think even your great-uncle understands that, even if he does not like it—but if you could have whatever you wanted, if you could have your greatest wish, what would you be doing instead?"

"Promise you will not laugh?"

I did not promise. I merely gave him an offended look. The very idea—as though I could not be trusted not to laugh.

Will took a deep breath and spoke on the exhale. "I should like to join the military."

It was a good thing I had made no promise, because I did laugh.

"But that is . . . that is . . . preposterous!" I laughed some more.

"No, it is not."

"But you are only sixteen!" I laughed even harder. "You are too young!"

"No, I am not." His voice grew enthusiastic; his face became animated with excitement. "Do you know, Bet, that they have tents at fairs, stalls in the streets—all you need do is go to one of these places, say you are of age, and they will believe you. They *want* to believe you."

His words sobered me instantly, the idea that such an idiotically dangerous thing could be so ridiculously easy. But then I thought about it some more and pulled a face.

"Well, if it is that easy, then why don't you go enlist right now?"

I thought I had him. He was fine at talk. But when it came down to it, he was too scared to reach for what he wanted.

He gave a nod of his head toward the house, where his great-uncle snored by the dying fire inside. "Because of him," he said. "It would kill him if I left."

"You leave him all the time when you go to school," I scoffed.

"Not like this," he said. "When I go off to school, he has good reason to be sure that I will come back, and that when I come back I will be alive."

Now there was a cheerful thought.

And a sensitive one as well.

It gave me pause to think that, amidst all the lying and cheating and mischief and arson, Will had managed to grow quite a bit of compassion for other people.

"I am all he has left," Will went on.

I was tempted to point out that his great-uncle had me also but I did know that it wasn't quite the same thing. Family was not something that could be replaced, as I well knew. And whatever else I might be to the old man—helper, reader, on some days even friend—I was not family.

Will confirmed as much by adding, "I did try to raise the issue with him last time I was home—I thought perhaps I could join the military in the usual fashion, go to an appropriate training school first before entering into the service—but I had to stop when he became upset. 'Don't you realize you are my only remaining relative? If something happened to you, I would die.'" Will attempted a casual shrug but couldn't quite pull it off. "It was awful."

It *was* awful, to think of the old man so upset. But it was also awful, perhaps even more so, to think of people not pursuing the things they wanted most in life.

I had one dream in this world, wanted one thing: the chance to be at school. Will had that thing I wanted most, and yet he valued it cheaply, dreamed of something else. Was there not some way Will and I could both achieve our dreams?

I was thankful that Will was so dejected about the hopelessness of his situation that, for once, he remained silent long enough to allow me time to think. That was the thing whenever Will was home: it was wonderful having his energy fill up the musty corners of the house, bring life back to the old place, but his energy *did* fill it up, entirely, so there was little space for anything *but* Will.

But now . . .

I asked myself the question again: Was there not some way both Will and I could achieve our dreams?

And within that blessed silence, I began to see the glimmering of an idea, which fast formed into a full-fledged plan.

Could we . . . ? If we both agreed . . . ?

As the excitement grew in me, I began to find fault with my own idea. For one thing, it could never work. For another thing, and perhaps more important in terms of my own vanity, Will would no doubt laugh in my face. If he, as evidenced earlier, did not like to be laughed at, I liked it even less. When you possess little in the world except your own pride, it is an awful thing to have it taken from you.

But what was I talking about? Why let pride stand in the way of what I wanted? And why give up and declare a thing impossible before even trying?

I *had* to try.

But before that, I did still have to point out, breaking the silence:

"You do realize war is stupid?" I said, eyes narrowing at Will.

"I do know that girls think that," he allowed.

"And girls are *right.*" I paused. "Still . . ."

"Still *what,* Bet?" he prompted when I did not speak for a long time.

Considering how often males were the center of attention in the household, never mind in the greater world, it was nice to feel as though I could occupy that place as well, when I had a mind to.

"Let's see," I said. "You want something I don't understand and have no use for—to go to war. And I want something you think is silly and do not want—to get an education. Have I got that right?"

Will shrugged, looking perplexed and even a trifle annoyed at what he no doubt regarded as my pointless statement of the obvious: facts of life that could never be changed. "I suppose."

"Perhaps," I said, feeling the smile stretch across my face, "there is a way we can help one another out."

CHAPTER *two*

Will called me Bet because when we first met he hadn't been able to say Elizabeth. For my part, I could not say Will and called him Ill instead, but whereas he was allowed to keep his nickname for me, I was hastily dissuaded from using mine for him.

We set eyes on each other for the first time when we were four years old, even though we had lived under the same roof since we were born, Will screaming his way into the world just a month before me.

I had no memory of Will's parents, but I had seen paintings of them in Paul Gardener's home.

Will's father, Frederick Gardener, had been that most masculine of clichés, tall, dark, and handsome, like his only son, and he had made his personal fortune in the import-export business. His wife, Victoria, was also tall, but there all physical similarities between husband and wife ended. In her portrait, Will's mother had hair the color of honey shot with gold, and eyes that looked as though the artist had borrowed parts of a summer sky to re-create them. And where Frederick looked as though he was at least trying to maintain some appearance of seriousness, Victoria had a smile that was broad, open, and generous.

Occasionally, Will would talk about that earlier house we'd both lived in: what ways it was the same, what ways different from the house we later lived in with Paul Gardener. But his reminiscences—of croquet mallets strewn across the lawn, of a nursery crammed full of decorations and toys, not to mention of the kind nanny that went with it all—were for me like hearing about a country I had never traveled to. For myself, I remembered with clarity only one small part of that house, and that a part that Will had never seen. I had also been in Frederick Gardener's study and one other part of the house, or so I'd been told of the latter—the wide foyer on the one and only occasion I crossed the threshold of that house—but I was exiting rather than entering, leaving that house for the last time, my face pressed into the shoulder of the person carrying me, and so I had no memory of what I was leaving behind me.

Will's father had been a handsome and successful businessman, his mother a beautiful society matron who could afford to choose whether to be kind or not. Who had been my mother?

Why, she had been the maid, of course.

My father? I had no idea. Nor was there anyone left alive who could tell me.

In all my memories of my mother—and I am sorry to say there are not many, and there are fewer and fewer as the years move on—she is impossibly young. Becky Smith was pretty in a way that was wholly different from Victoria Gardener's expensive beauty. My mother was tiny and dark—I can only assume I inherited my great height from my father—and she was always busy, busy, doing whatever was required of her to help the household run smoothly. I would glimpse her briefly in the still-dark early hours of the morning when she rose from our shared bed to start her day, and at the end of that long day when she fell back into bed, exhausted. Occasionally, if she could steal a few minutes, she would visit me in between. The rest of the time, particularly when I was very small, other servants took turns attending to my various needs.

I understood, from having overheard the conversations of others, that when my mother "got herself into trouble," as the saying goes, there had been some talk of putting her out on the street. It would have been the usual thing for a family like the Gardeners to do. What use was a maid who suffered bouts of morning sickness? Why should a respectable household even consider keeping on a maid who had been foolish enough to get herself in the family way with no husband in sight? It would be unseemly. It was unheard-of.

And yet, to Victoria Gardener at least, it was not unheard-of. Perhaps her own condition, being with child, made her more sensitive to her maid's? Perhaps that made her more empathetic than other women of her position in society would have been, and she could imagine how frightening it would be to be pregnant and alone and suddenly find oneself put out on the street with no hope of a better prospect? Whatever her reasoning, she made the kindly decision, prevailing upon her husband to go along with it, to let the maid stay. So long as Becky Smith kept her baby confined to the servants' quarters at the top of the house, so long as the household itself was not disturbed in any discernible way, Will and I were to be allowed to grow up under the same roof.

Later on, when I learned what had happened, it was odd to think of Will and me living our early years in the same house, never seeing each other, our experiences of that house so vastly different. Will told me later that he had been happy back then, and I believed him. For myself, my few memories indicated that I had been happy too. There was food to eat, a place to sleep, I was cared for when people had the time—what other life had I ever known?

And then the typhoid came.

Typhoid is a fever contracted from consuming food or water that has been colonized by bacteria. I knew this from reading I'd done on the subject when I was old enough to become curious.

Typhoid causes a very high and sustained fever, an enormous amount of sweating, stomach disturbances, and diarrhea. The progression of the disease is typically four weeks, the four different stages of it distinguishing each week.

In the first week, the patient experiences a steadily increasing temperature, general tiredness, persistent headache and cough. There may be hemorrhaging from the nose, and even the eyes, and many experience abdominal pain.

During the second week, the fever elevates to a level of approximately 104 degrees Fahrenheit and remains there for quite some time. Delirium is frequent at this stage, and the patient sometimes becomes quite agitated. In approximately one-third of patients, rose-colored spots appear on the lower chest and abdomen. Labored sounds can be heard from the lungs and abdomen, the latter becoming distended and painful. The spleen and liver also become enlarged, and the diarrhea can be green and awful.

Over the course of the third week of illness, a number of complications may set in: intestinal hemorrhage, intestinal perforation, encephalitis or acute inflammation of the brain, abscesses.

In the fourth and final week, the fever remains very high, extreme dehydration occurs, and the patient becomes almost constantly delirious.

Sometimes, somewhere during all that misery, the patient dies.

Not always, but often enough.

I could talk about typhoid only in a medical-textbook sort of way, as I have done here, for to do any differently would mean dwelling on memories that were too painful to think of.

The typhoid took Will's parents.

The typhoid took my mother.

In the beginning, I did not understand what was happening to her. Well, in truth, for the entire month that followed, I did not understand. All I knew was that my mother, with her special sunny smile that she reserved for me, was no longer waking in the still-dark hours of the morning to start her workday. In fact, she could not even get out of bed.

The other servants tried to keep me from her—whether because they did not want me to see her in such a state or because they feared I would get the illness as well, I could not say. She was kept quarantined, as Will's parents were quarantined in their own far more spacious section of the house. I was ordered to sleep with one of the other servants.

But I would sneak out in the middle of the night when everyone else was sleeping to visit her.

Sometimes, seeing her in her delirium, I did not even recognize her *as* my mother. I did not understand half of what she said. But I could yet remember what her smile looked like, what it felt like to have her hand touch my cheek, and so I would crawl into bed beside her, my body clinging to her feverish one.

We were like that one night when her breathing labored once more, then slowed, then stopped, and I felt that seemingly eternal fever finally leave her as the cold settled into her body.

They told me later that when they found us in the morning, my small arms were gripped around her stiff neck so tightly, they had to pry me from her.

On the face of things, there were some startling coincidences between my life and Will's: the way his parents and my mother had died, our close birthdays, even the way we looked. Paul Gardener liked to say that there were no accidents in life, that everything happened out of choice or through design, that everything happened for a reason. But from where I sat, so much of life did seem accidental, haphazard. How else to explain why one person lived while another died? How else to explain why one was born a boy, one a girl, one into the upper class, one into a substantially lower social stratum, the fortunes and futures of both dictated wholly by things over which they had no control? If there was any choice or design in that, I couldn't see it.

After the deaths of Frederick and Victoria Gardener, it was

decided that Will would go live with his great-uncle, Paul Gardener. It was not just because he was the only relative remaining who shared Will's last name, but also because all of Victoria's relatives taken together could not come close to Paul Gardener's wealth. He had the best kind of fortune: a family fortune.

When Paul Gardener, not yet an old man, came to collect his charge and settle affairs at the house, which was to be sold, he took some time to talk to the staff. They needed letters of recommendation, as they now had to seek new employment. Will was present at the time, and he told me later about the exchange that transpired between his great-uncle and one of the servants.

Paul Gardener was in his nephew Frederick's study, going through the dead man's bills, when a servant came in bearing tea on a tray.

"I hope you will be able to find a suitable placement," he said, addressing the servant with kindness. "I would gladly give all of you positions in my own home, but I fear the old place is already overstaffed as it is."

"Thank you, sir. I'll manage."

"My nephew and his wife—they were the only ones unfortunate enough to succumb to the typhoid?"

"Oh, no, sir. One other died as well." When Will would tell this part of the story, I always pictured the servant shrugging as he said what came next, as though the other life lost was of little matter. "It was just one of the maids."

"I see. That is hard. And it must be very hard on the poor maid's remaining family."

"Oh, but she had none. Unless of course you include her daughter."

"A daughter!"

"Yes, sir. An orphan now, though, since she is no longer anyone's daughter."

"What has been done with her?"

"Oh, she is still here. Well, but not for long. The proper authorities—"

"Bring her to me," he commanded.

A moment later, I entered Paul Gardener's life; I, with my downturned eyes and my old brown dress. Out of the corner of one of those downturned eyes, I glimpsed a boy, the first I'd seen outside of pictures in the books my mother had occasionally borrowed from the Gardeners' vast library. The boy was about my age, I thought, and wearing knee pants.

At that time, Paul Gardener was clear-sighted and vigorous, nothing like the man he would be twelve years later.

He came down to my height, bending on one knee with ease and not exhibiting any of the creakiness that would plague him later in life. He reached out his hand to me slowly, as though trying not to startle a skittish animal, and with gentle fingers raised my chin so that we were eye to eye.

"What is your name, child?"

"It is Elizabeth, sir."

"Elizabeth," he said softly. "A fine name. Perhaps someone fancied that one day you would be a queen." He paused. "Do you know what is to be done with you, Elizabeth, now that your mother is . . . no longer here?"

I met his steady gaze. My mother had taught me to use precision when answering adults, and I sought to do so now. "They say I am to go to an orphanage, sir."

"An orphanage!" He barked a laugh but it did not sound to me as though he was genuinely amused. "The workhouse, more like."

I did not know to what he was referring, but from his expression I guessed it was no place I would ever want to go.

"Tell me, Elizabeth," he said, his voice gentle once again. "If I gave you a choice between going to this . . . *orphanage* place or coming back with me and the boy to live in my house, which would you choose?"

I bit my lip. I was not used to choosing anything for myself. I thought about the fact that the orphanage—or workhouse, as he called it—was a complete unknown to me while this man seemed kind, and the boy looked like he had the potential to be . . . interesting.

Despite my mother's advice to always speak precisely, I still had trouble with my *w*'s, so when I spoke, my words came out: "I 'ill go with you, sir."

Paul Gardener laughed. "I can see you have a bit of trouble pronouncing some of your letters." He looked at the boy with a twinkle in his eye, but when he next spoke, his words carried a jolly teasing in them and not a cruel one. "She has difficulty with *w*'s, while you have trouble with words of too many syllables. But already, boy, she speaks better than you."

It was then—as I realized for the first time that I would never see my mother's face again, would soon leave behind the only home I had ever known, and for what, I did not know—that I started to cry. I don't think I had fully understood until that moment that my entire world had changed in irreversible ways. The shock of it filled me with sadness and fear like nothing I had ever experienced.

And so it was that Paul Gardener picked me up in his arms and carried me out of the study and through the foyer I had never seen. I did not see it then either, for my face was buried in his shoulder.

Grangefield Hall was a far larger home than the one we had come from, or at least that was what Will told me. Since I had never properly seen the outside of the home I had lived in before, I had nothing by which to gauge this new place, although the outside did look impressively large, with all its stone and turrets and ivy. The inside did seem a lot bigger than what I'd been used to; certainly the bedroom I was led to was bigger than the place I used to sleep.

That bedroom was on the third floor. On the floor below me, I was told, were Paul Gardener's rooms and Will's, while above me were the servants' quarters. It felt odd having a room all to myself; before, I had always shared. The room, which I was told had been one of the guest rooms, was decorated in a sober and masculine manner. Not that I minded; my old room had been decorated in a mostly empty manner.

"Do not worry," Paul Gardener advised, "I will have someone in to redecorate the room so it is more suitable for a girl." He regarded my brown dress. "And we will see that you get some new clothes as well."

Embarrassed at the idea that he might pity me, I tried to hide one worn boot by covering its top with the other. But I was too late.

"Shoes too," Paul Gardener added, leaving me to get used to my new surroundings.

If material possessions really did bring joy, then in losing my mother, I had gained a little bit of heaven.

But from where I was sitting, it did not seem to be an even trade.

Will had to teach me how to play.

I realize how odd that sounds. Imagine that: a child who didn't know how to play. But back at his parents' house, my "play" had only ever involved helping the servants with chores a small child was capable of helping with—standing on a stool and drying pots and pans, dusting the servants' quarters, polishing the silver. Of the last, I could remove the tarnish from a soupspoon so well that the queen could delight in viewing her image on its curved surface. But give me a ball or a proper toy or even a doll? I had no idea what to do with such things.

"Kick it, Bet!" Will shouted across the lawn at me as I stood there, watching the ball roll by. "You're supposed to kick it back to me!"

"Why?" I asked.

"So then I can kick it back to you!"

"And then I suppose I'll be expected to kick it to you a second time?"

Will nodded eagerly.

"What's the point?" I asked.

A puzzled look came over Will's face. "I dunno," he said. "Most people think it's rather fun."

"Fun." The word seemed so foreign to me, the very concept unimaginable. *"Fun."*

Then, seeing Will's crestfallen look and wanting to please him, I trotted up to the ball, tentatively drew one leg back, and kicked it toward him.

My God, I thought, *that* was *fun.*

And when, sure as night following day, Will kicked it back to me, and it was once again my turn to kick it to him, I struck the ball with my foot much harder.

That harder strike felt even better.

It was as though all the anger that had been in me—and for the first time I realized that I *was* filled with anger, anger at the universe for taking my mother, anger over the unfairness of pretty much everything—was briefly released from my body with the force of that kick.

"You are good at this!" Will said, chasing after the ball, which had shot right past him. "I think maybe you have played this game before!"

"No!" I laughed, surprised at the sound of laughter coming out of my body, surprised at how good and joyful I suddenly felt. "But I think I like it!"

Will and I became friends that day.

For the next six years, we played together as friends—equals, even—with Paul Gardener often observing us from his study window or, on nice days, from the fieldstone patio out back.

Then, when I was ten, one of Victoria Gardener's relatives came to visit, as they did from time to time in order to check on Will's progress. She sat beside the master of the house on the patio in her wide-brimmed hat, the two of them sipping lemonade as Will and I played a spirited game of croquet under the hot summer sun. I never could figure out if she spoke at a near shout because she was hard of hearing or because she wanted to be overheard. Whatever the case, her words reached us with ease.

"I understand, Paul, your having permitted the children to play with each other when they were younger. And it is to your Christian credit that you were kind enough to take in that wretched child rather than let her go to the workhouse. But do you not realize how . . . *wrong* it is to allow them to continue so casually in one another's company?"

If she *was* hard of hearing, the old man was not of a mind to accommodate her infirmity, because when he spoke—and I was sure he did, for I saw his lips move—it was impossible to hear what he said.

"No, *you* don't understand," the woman said. "Yes, Victoria was kind enough to let the maid continue in service, but you must realize, she never intended for the *maid's child* to be raised with her *son*."

More silent words from the old man.

"Surely you can see how . . . *unseemly* this all is," the woman went on, growing more heated by the moment. "What's more, you are raising unrealistic expectations in that girl. Treat her like an equal, like one of the family, and she will grow up believing that one day a life like this could be hers. Now I ask you: Can you imagine any young man of Will's stature *ever* considering marrying a girl who was a maid's bastard? Really, Paul, you do that girl no favors."

To this, the master of the house said nothing.

It was decided that since Will was ten, he would be sent away to school. He would still visit during semester breaks and over the summer, but he really was old enough to go now, his education paramount.

As for me, after six years of blissful playing, I was now to assume more responsibilities around Grangefield Hall. No, I was not to be moved to the servants' quarters, although I believe some of them felt I should be, but it was expected that I would take on chores: I would do mending, I would help out when any of the other servants was sick, I would polish the silver—I had made the mistake of admitting a proficiency at that task—and, of course, I would read to the master whenever asked.

My fortunes and Will's had been intertwined for six years, but now our lives diverged: he was to receive a proper education, while I was to assume a life somewhere between resident and servant.

Just as my bedroom was located on a floor between the entitled inhabitants of the house below me and the servants above, I lived between worlds, not quite family, not quite servant, neither fish nor fowl.

I was grateful to Paul Gardener, whom I always addressed as sir, never Mr. Gardener, and whom I always thought of by his full name or as the old man or the master of the house or simply the master. I even loved him a little. If not for him and the generosity he had shown me, I would have been sent to the workhouse.

But Paul Gardener was not my family, and neither was Will.

And Grangefield Hall was not my home.

CHAPTER *three*

"Are you *insane,* Bet?"

Not exactly the reaction I'd been hoping for when I made my proposal to Will, I'll grant you. Still, I tried to tell myself it was a start. At least my idea was now out there, loose in the world.

Turn the clock back a minute or two . . .

"Perhaps," I said, feeling the smile stretch across my face, "there is a way we can help one another out."

"Such as?"

"You will go into the military, while I will take your place at school."

"Don't be daft," Will scoffed. Then he added, in an effort to humor me or out of genuine curiosity, I couldn't tell: "I understand the part about me going into the military, which I suppose could be accomplished if I were willing to deliver unto Uncle an emotional deathblow, but how could you possibly take my place at school?"

"First off," I said, "you wouldn't be dealing him a deathblow. On the contrary, that would be the purpose of my taking your place at school. So long as *someone* named Will Gardener reports to school, your great-uncle will never know what you've done. As to the question of how I could possibly take your place at school, the answer should be obvious: by becoming you." I added smugly, feeling rather pleased with myself, "By becoming *a boy.*"

It was this last that brought us to:

"Are you *insane,* Bet?"

He seemed so convinced of that possibility, I gave it a moment's serious consideration.

"No," I at last concluded. "Or, rather, I may be insane about some things, but I think I'm seeing this quite clearly. We each want something, and it's my belief that if we're willing to work really hard, we can both get what we want."

"And how do you propose to go about *becoming a boy?*" Will's exasperation with me was growing by the second. "What are you going to do? Cut your hair? Wear a suit?"

I reflected. "Yes, I suppose I'll have to do both those things eventually, won't I?" I didn't mind the suit part so much—the idea of wearing masculine clothing struck me as liberating—but giving up my hair would be hard. It was the only thing about myself I regularly thought pretty.

"Even if you do those things, people will still know you're a girl."

"How so?"

Will waved his hand at my body, toe to crown, blushing furiously all the while. "Your body, for one thing. You have a woman's body, Bet." More furious blushing. "Or at least a girl's."

Now it was my turn to blush. I had never thought of Will noticing that I was different from him in that manner. Still, I was determined. "Then I will find a way to . . . *disguise* my shape."

"But then there will be the matter of your voice, and after that, the matter of your walk, and after that . . ." He paused. "Really, Bet, do you not see? No matter what you do, no matter how much you change, there will always be one more thing you haven't taken into consideration. I'm sorry, but this harebrained scheme of yours can't possibly work."

"All I *see,* Will, is a boy who is unwilling to do what it takes to get what he wants out of life."

"That hurts, Bet." It was impossible to tell whether he was being sincere or sarcastic. For my part, I chose to treat it as though it was the former.

"Not as much as going through life without getting the opportunity to live your dream. Not as much as knowing that there are things you could do to achieve that dream but choose not to."

"You are wearing me down."

"Good."

"It's not like I have anything better to do with my summer."

"Exactly! Look at it as an adventure! Look at it as a game! Your task, Will Gardener, is to help me transform myself into you."

He laughed then, recovering his good humor for just a moment before becoming sober again.

"It is impossible," he said. "This thing you want to do—it can never work."

What Will didn't count on was that I could be fierce when I wanted to.

"At least," I countered just as soberly, "we can try."

That night I stayed up late, thinking of all that would need to be accomplished over the next few months and making a list. The following day I hurried through my chores and then looked all over the house for Will. At last I located him on the lawn. He was sitting under a tree, his back against its trunk, reading a book and chomping on an apple.

I approached and stood nervously above him, waiting for him to notice me.

When he failed to look up, I cleared my throat. Loudly.

"I know you are there," he said, turning the page, "because you're blocking the sun, but I want to finish this chapter. I only have a page left."

I waited. Impatiently.

"There," he said at last, leaving a finger inside the book to mark his place.

"I am ready to begin," I said, feeling nerves overtake me again.

"Begin what?"

"Why, my transformation!"

"Into . . . ?"

"Into you, of course. Into a boy."

Will groaned. "You're still going on about that? I thought for sure a night's sleep would bring you to your senses."

"Well, it has not. I am more determined than ever. *In fact,* I spent last night making a list of everything that needs to be done."

"You really aren't going to let this go, are you?"

I waved my sheet of paper at him insistently.

"Very well." He sighed, finally putting the book down and gesturing impatiently with his fingers for the paper. "Let me see what you have there."

I handed over the sheet and moved to stand behind him so I could read over his shoulder.

– Walking
– Talking
– Handwriting
– Clothes

"You left out the part about the hair," he pointed out.

"I keep forgetting that part. I will add it later."

He looked up at me, a disturbing, scathing expression on his face. "It took you all night to come up with four words?" he asked me.

I felt a flush reddening my cheeks. "A lot of serious thinking and planning went on between those four words."

"Yes, so much thinking and planning you forgot about the hair."

"I will remember when the time comes."

"Being a boy involves more than items on a list." He thrust the sheet back at me in disgust. "And even if you do manage to make all these changes, even if you manage to turn yourself into a boy, you will never exactly be me. When you go to school—I laugh at the very idea!—you will not be Will Gardener."

"But why should that matter?" I countered.

"Excuse me?"

"You are to start, yet again, at a new school this fall. Will Gardener is just a name to the people there until a body comes to attach itself to that name. But no one will have any expectations of what Will Gardener should look like. So what does it matter if I can't exactly become you, so long as I can persuade people that I am you?"

"Huh." Will looked dumbfounded. "I hadn't thought of that."

"You see?" I was extraordinarily pleased with myself. "Already I am smarter than a boy."

"Very well." Will sighed. "Where shall we begin?"

"That suit doesn't look like that when I wear it, does it?" Will asked, scratching his head.

"No," I admitted ruefully, regarding my reflection in the looking glass. "It does not."

Everything about it was wrong: the way the shirt accentuated my breasts, the way the shoulders of the jacket were too broad for my slimmer frame, the way the waistband of the trousers hung too low on my hips, even the length of the sleeves and trousers. I had always thought I was the same size as Will, but clearly, I saw now, I had been deluding myself. The sleeves were so long only the tips of my fingers showed, while the hems of the trousers pooled around my naked feet.

We were in my bedroom. Will had loaned me one of his suits to try on, waiting outside while I changed, of course.

"I figured," Will said, the tone of his voice suggesting that he was still merely humoring me and did not share my wholehearted faith in my plan, "that once I'm in the military, I won't need my suits, so you could have a few of them to take off with you to school." He could not prevent a laugh from escaping at the sight of me in the looking glass, my body looking ridiculous in his clothes. "No," he went on, having regained control of himself, "this will never do. I suppose you'll just have to give up."

"Give up?"

"Of course. What else can you do? I can't very well take you to my tailor, can I, and have him make a man's suit for you?"

Even I could see the futility in such a course of action. If we tried doing that, no doubt the tailor would report the peculiarity to Will's great-uncle.

"No, of course not," I admitted.

"So that's it, then." Will looked so smug, I could almost see him mentally washing his hands of the whole affair as he made to leave the room.

"No, it is not," I said, my words stopping him as he put his hand on the doorknob.

"It isn't?" He looked puzzled.

What did he think, that I was going to give up so easily? That I was going to simply quit at the very first obstacle?

"Get me my sewing kit," I commanded him.

"Your—?"

"My sewing kit," I said impatiently. "You know, that thing with threads and needles?"

"I know what a sewing kit is."

"Well then?" I prodded him. "I can't very well traipse through the house looking like this, can I? You'll find it in the basket near the fireplace down in the drawing room."

Perhaps too stunned by my authoritarian manner to offer any rebuttal, Will obeyed.

"Thank you," I said imperiously when he returned with the requested item. I opened the kit and removed a box of straight pins. "Here." I placed the box in Will's hand. Then I dragged a chair to the center of the room and proceeded to climb up on top of it.

"What am I supposed to do with these?" Will asked, shaking the box of pins at me.

"I can't do everything myself! And I certainly can't pin up clothes properly when I'm wearing them. The hems would come out all uneven."

"You want me to pretend to be a dressmaker's assistant and pin up the hems for you?"

"*Nooo.* I want you to pretend to be a tailor's assistant and pin up the hems for me. Is that too much to ask? Once you accomplish that, I'll do all the rest."

"You're impossible," he muttered, but at least he got down on his knees and, squinting at the fabric, folded up the hems of the trousers so he could begin placing pins at regular intervals.

"Thank you," I said.

"I'm only doing this to shut you up."

"You shouldn't talk with pins in your mouth. And anyway, I wasn't thanking you for doing what I asked."

Will stopped for a moment, looked up at me. "What, then?"

"I was thanking you for calling me impossible." I smiled down at him. "I rather like the idea of being impossible."

"Girls."

"Boys. Now get back to work."

But when Will finished pinning the material at my wrists and ankles so that I could properly hem them later, my reflection still looked wrong. And not just because of my breasts.

"I still need to fix the waistband," I said, "so it doesn't hang so low on my hips. Here." I handed him a couple of pins. Then I took off the jacket and, turning away from him, lifted up the waistband of the trousers to a level that looked about right. "If you place a few of these in the back so that the whole is tighter, I can sew darts there later."

I was just beginning to think that Will was getting rather good at obeying instructions when I felt a pin stab me.

"Ouch!" I shouted, whirling on him. "You did that on purpose!"

"Would I do that to you?" His expression was innocent. Too innocent.

"Well, hurry up," I grumbled. "We have a lot more to do."

"More?"

"Of course, more! You don't expect me to go off to school with just one suit, do you?"

❦

"Can you write out the alphabet for me, Will?" I asked one night, having followed Will out to the back garden after dinner.

"If you can't even make your letters," Will said with a snort, "how do you ever expect to go away to school?"

"I know how to make my letters, Will Gardener! And you know that I know. But my hand is a girl's hand. When you send me notes from school, your hand is less florid than mine. If I am to convince people that I am—"

"Fine." Will made no effort to hide his exasperation. "Get me paper and pen."

"Uppercase *and* lowercase," I directed as he began to write.

"You take this all so seriously," he muttered. "One would think you actually believe you're going to get your way."

Normally, I would have responded with heat to a remark like that. But I was too busy being shocked at what I was seeing.

"Do you always hold your hand like that when you make your letters?" I asked.

Will looked up. "How do you mean?"

"Like that." I gestured with my hand. "Your fingers are all cramped down tight together near the nib. It looks most uncomfortable." A thought occurred to me. "No wonder the writing in your notes always looks so crabbed!"

"My handwriting is not crabbed!"

I ignored him.

Without asking permission, I took the pen from his hand. Then, forcing my fingers into the impossible death grip I'd seen him use a moment ago, I put pen to paper. The result of my efforts was something that didn't look even remotely like my usual pretty hand.

"Huh," I said, pleased with myself. "Well, that was easy."

"It may be easy enough to imitate a boy's handwriting," Will pointed out the next day as we played croquet, "although I don't see why you seem to feel that girls write so much better than boys, but talking is different. It's a lot harder to fake what people hear than what they read."

"Oh, really?"

"Yes. As a matter of fact, I will wager money on it."

"Too bad I haven't got any."

"No, of course not. I'm sorry." Will at least had the good grace to look embarrassed. But not for long. "Very well, then," he went on, brightening, "if I win, you give up your harebrained scheme and admit it can never work."

That would be a hard bet to make, I thought. If I wagered and lost, my sense of honor would force me to hold up my end of the bargain. But I hated seeing him look so cocky, and he would look even cockier if I did not accept the bet.

"Fine," I said. "But if *I* win, you need to throw your wholehearted support behind me *and* you have to read to your great-uncle at least once a week."

"Wait a second! Why do you get two things to my one?"

"Because I'm smart enough to ask for more? Because the old man might as well get something out of this too? Because if you're so sure you're going to win, it shouldn't matter to you how many things I ask for?"

His mouth tightened, but at last he put out his hand. "Fine," he said through clenched teeth.

I shook his hand, hard. "Fine," I returned with a smile.

❦

That night after dinner, the master asked me to read to him for a little while, as was his habit. Perhaps obsessed with his advancing years and how little of life remained ahead of him, he wanted me to read from *King Lear* again.

"'Meantime we shall express our darker purpose.'" I began the passage where Lear talks about dividing his kingdom in three.

"Doesn't she read beautifully?" The old man turned toward Will.

"Yes, she does." Will was practically sputtering. "But whose voice was that? She sounded like . . . *you!*"

"Isn't it marvelous? She can do all sorts of voices: male, female, old, young, rich, poor. I suppose it comes from years of reading to me. Why, there are times I feel as though I will never need to attend the theater again, since having Elizabeth here is like having a live performance every night!" His expression grew puzzled. "Have you never noticed what a talent she has for this?"

"No." Will was practically seething now. "I have not."

"With your permission, sir," I asked the old man, "might I be allowed to read a little from *Macbeth* instead?" Before he could question why I wanted to do this, I added, "I feel that that play might best show off to Will my range of voices."

"Of course, child."

"'When shall we three meet again / In thunder, lightning, or in rain?'"

"You see?" the old man said to his great-nephew. "That's the first of the three Witches. And listen to Elizabeth: she sounds just like a crone!"

"Yes," Will observed dryly. "She does."

I took the liberty of skipping ahead to the third scene and Macbeth's entrance.

"'So foul and fair a day I have not seen.'" I read the words of one of the most hated and misunderstood men in all of literature.

"And now she sounds like a young man!" the old man crowed proudly, as though he were responsible for my talent.

"Yes, she does." Will stared at me as something struck him. "She sounds like *me.*"

"That's funny," the old man said. "I never noticed that before, but you are right. When Elizabeth does young men's voices, she does sound like you."

"Perhaps," I said, smiling at Will, "I am so good at it because I have spent so many years listening to you talk and talk and talk."

Will had never hit me, but I got the feeling he would have liked to do nothing more right then.

"Here you go," I said, rising from my seat and carrying the book over to Will. "Perhaps you would like to read to your great-uncle tonight? If you practice a bit, you can become equally adept at imitating other people's voices."

Before he could reply, I sauntered from the room.

"You walk like a girl!" Will shouted at me.

"That's probably because I *am* a girl!" I shouted right back at him.

"Yes, I do know that, Bet. But you sway too much when you walk."

"I sway?"

"Yes, sway! Those . . . *hips* of yours. They swish back and forth. It is fine for a girl but—"

"Not for a boy. Very well." I gave a firm nod of my head. "Show me, then."

"Well, it's like this." Will demonstrated as we stood on the lawn. "You must walk—no, you must *stride* as though you have some great purpose in mind."

"You look ridiculous," I said, watching him walk back and forth. "You look like you're off to execute somebody."

"Exactly. That's what I mean about purpose. But there are other times when you need to adopt a more casual approach, as though you're out for a stroll without a care in the world."

This he demonstrated as well.

"What are you doing with your hands in your pockets?" I asked.

"I'm jangling my change, counting it sometimes. It's what men do when they stroll."

"If you haven't a care in the world," I said with a snort, "I don't see why you'd be worrying about how much money you have."

"Laugh all you want to, but while you're laughing, practice, practice, practice."

I obeyed. At least he was finally getting into the spirit of the thing.

"And no swishing!" he shouted after me as I paraded up and down the lawn, seeking to adopt a more masculine stride.

When he felt I'd done enough swishless walking for one day, he called for a maid.

"Lemonade?" I asked, hoping that was what he was going to request. It was hot out.

"No," he said to me. "Cutting shears, please," he said to the maid.

"Cutting shears?" I wanted to know what he was up to.

After the maid had brought the requested item and safely departed, Will reached out and, with one quick motion, snipped off a lock of my hair.

"Hey! What did you do that for?" I demanded, my hand instinctively reaching to protect the rest of my hair.

"I'm going to need this," Will said, "in order to have the wig maker fashion you a wig to use after you cut the rest of your hair off." Will smiled. "After all, there will still be times when you'll need to look like a girl, won't there?"

Allowing my hair to be cut was one of the hardest things I'd ever had to do.

Funny, I usually thought of being a girl as something that had mostly just gotten in my way all my life. And yet, watching my hair grow progressively shorter as lock after lock fell to the bathroom floor, I felt as though I were losing a part of myself that I hadn't previously recognized as precious.

Somehow, it made me feel slightly better that, although I had to lose my hair, Will was the one doing the cutting.

"Tell me about school," I said to Will, hoping to take my mind off what was happening as tears of loss sprang to my eyes. "What's it like?"

"Probably a lot more boring than you imagine," Will said, concentrating on his task. *Snip, snip.* "A bunch of high-spirited boys." *Snip, snip.* "A handful of stern masters." *Snip, snip.* "Lousy food."

"Do you think I'm smart enough?"

The shears ceased their snipping and Will's eyes met mine in the mirror. He did not comment on how rare it was for me to show such insecurity, and for this I was grateful. He did not comment on the tears in my eyes, and I was grateful for this too.

"You're smarter than any boy I've ever known, Bet," he said, looking wholly serious for once.

"Right, then." I closed my eyes briefly to stop the tears. When I opened them again and spoke, my voice was stern. "Keep cutting."

Snip, snip. Snip, snip, snip.

Before I knew it, it was done. My long hair was all gone.

Will bent down so that his head was beside mine in the mirror.

"We used to look so much alike," I said, "that we could have been taken for brother and sister."

"But now," Will said, "we look like brother and brother."

Then Will produced the wig he'd had made for me and dropped it on my head at a skewed angle. "Good thing you've got this."

I straightened the wig so it sat properly on my head.

"And now"—I smiled at myself—"I'm a girl again."

"Must be nice to be able to go back and forth like that," Will said.

❦

"Are you going to let me in or aren't you?" Will shouted through the locked door of my bedroom.

"Hold on! Hold on!" I shouted back. "Almost ready!"

A moment later, I let him in. "Voilà!" I said, taking a step backward.

I studied his amazed expression as he regarded me in my black suit, the black suit that used to be his black suit.

He blushed as he gestured vaguely at the part of my body where my breasts used to be. "How did you make . . . *those* disappear?"

"I need to maintain some mysteries, don't I?" I answered saucily.

It would have been awkward talking to Will about what I'd done to my breasts. In truth, I'd used fabric to bind them. It was uncomfortable, but no more so than the corset I'd had to wear.

"And . . . *that.*" Will blushed more furiously still as he gestured at the bulge I'd created in the front of my trousers. "It shouldn't look so big . . . *that.*"

"Oh!" It was my turn to blush. "Sorry!" Then I commanded him to leave the room again so I could remove one of the two pairs of stockings I'd shoved down my trousers. I should have known that just one pair would do.

"Is that better?" I asked, letting him in again.

"Much," he said, looking relieved. "But that tie . . ."

"Tie?" My hand went to my throat. "What's the matter with my tie? It's the one you gave me."

"But it's all wrong." Will approached me. "May I?"

"Please."

Will undid the tie I'd so carefully knotted. "The thing you need to remember at all times," Will said, as he folded one end over the other, "is that a balance must always be struck. Tie it too loosely, and the masters will have your head, but tie it too tightly, as you had it, and you'll be a laughingstock."

He led me to the mirror. "Do you see what I mean?"

Will was right. His way made a huge difference, all the difference in the world: it was the perfect balance between studious and rakish. At last, I looked as though I might belong . . . *somewhere.*

"Can you show me how to tie it like you just did?" I asked him.

He stood behind me so I could watch what he was doing in the mirror. He seemed so patient now, and he remained so as I practiced.

"Have I got it?" I asked, this time using my boy voice when I spoke.

"Yes," he said. "You're perfect now, Will Gardener."

Later on that night, we were out in the back garden, enjoying the August moon.

"In all your planning, Bet," Will said into the lazy silence, "you've left out one important item."

"I have?"

"Yes. If I go off to the military, and you take my place at school so that Uncle continues believing I am at school, what sort of excuse will you give for your own absence from here?"

CHAPTER *four*

"The *Better Man* Academy? Are you *joking,* Uncle?"

The old man appeared to be puzzled by this query.

"Joking?" he echoed. "Have you ever known me to *joke* about anything in my life?"

Will was forced to concede that he had not.

"At any rate," the old man continued, "it is not the *Better Man* Academy. It is the Betterman Academy."

"It still sounds to me like a joke," Will said, "a name that someone has made up." Will altered his voice to sound as though he were reading an advertisement for hair tonic from one of the newspapers: " 'Send your boy to us here at the Betterman Academy, and we will send you back a *Better Man!*' "

"Perhaps Betterman is the name of the gentleman who founded the academy?" I interjected—helpfully, I thought.

"Whatever it is named for, it still sounds nutty to me," Will muttered.

I wondered at his aggression toward the mere name of the school. After all, he wasn't the one who was going to be attending there. I was.

"Well," the old man said, "then you should have thought about that before you got yourself sent down from every reputable school within a reasonable radius of home."

"Is that why you chose it, then?" Will wondered. "For its proximity to home?"

"Hardly." The old man snorted. "It is still two days' journey from here. I *chose* it"—and here he paused, and then commenced to thunder—*"because it was the only place I could find that would take you!"*

August 7, 18—

Dear Miss Smith,

I write to you on behalf of my mother, Mrs. Henry Larwood. Having reviewed your application along with the many we have received, it is our decision that you would make the most fit companion for her as my husband and I commence our yearlong tour of the Orient. It is a great comfort for me to think that Mother will be tended to by such a caring girl. Mr. Gardener's letter of reference impressed us all greatly, and I must confess, Mother is particularly charmed that not only can you read to her daily, but you can do so using voices!

The compensation for your duties will be generous. You will have every other Sunday off. We realize that a single day will not be sufficient time for you to journey back to Grangefield Hall, and so, as you requested, you will be permitted a week's leave at the Christmas holidays and another week later in the spring. We will need you here no later than the first week of September. Should these terms meet with your approval, please reply with all speed to the above address.

"Is this woman mad?" the old man said after I'd read the letter to him, my hands shaking nervously all the while. In truth, I could have read the letter without looking at the page, since I'd written every word myself. "She talks about a letter of reference from Mr. Gardener. Well, *I* certainly never wrote to her!"

"No, sir," Will answered, using rare formality in addressing his great-uncle. Then he cleared his throat, his own nerves taking over. "The Mr. Gardener in the letter would be me."

"*You?* But I don't understand . . ."

"I wrote it," Will said. "Bet needed a letter of reference and I provided her with one."

"Yes, but I still don't understand any of this. Why—?"

Will opened his mouth to explain, but I stopped him. This had all been my idea, after all. Any grief that might come of it was my responsibility.

"I am sixteen years old now, sir," I said boldly. "Isn't it high time I made my way in the world?"

I would never have guessed, not in a million years, that the old man would look so crestfallen at the idea of my leave-taking.

"But I thought you were happy here, Elizabeth," he said. "Haven't we been good to you?"

"Of course!" I said brightly, hoping to erase any damage I'd caused. I tried on a happy laugh. "But I could not stay here forever, could I?" I sobered. "After all, I am not family. At some point, I will need to earn my own living. Is it not best that I start now, when I have an opportunity with someone who wants to employ me?"

"If it is about money . . . yes, I see where perhaps we have taken advantage of you all these years, not paying you. Perhaps we could—"

"It is not about money, sir," I said gently. "And I could never take yours. You have already given me so much."

"It is just simply time for Bet to become independent," Will interjected.

"*You* helped her in this," the old man accused Will.

"Yes," Will said, straightening his back, "and I would do it again.

People need, Uncle, to follow where their hearts and minds lead them." Will softened. "And as Mrs. Larwood's daughter's letter indicates, Bet will be home for the holidays. So it is not as though you will never see her again."

"And I will write to you, sir," I added. "I will write every week to tell you how I am getting on."

"But who will read those letters to me, Elizabeth, if you are busy somewhere else, reading to some*one* else?"

That hurt.

"I'm sure one of the servants would be happy to do so," Will said, stepping in to save me. "I'm sure they all would rather read letters to you than, oh, I don't know, polish the silver *one more time.*"

The old man smiled weakly at this attempt at humor.

"And isn't it fortunate," Will pressed on, encouraged by that weak smile, "why, look at the address on the letter!" Will blushed. "Well, no, of course you can't actually see it. But it is not far from the Betterman Academy, and they want Bet there very close to the day that I am due at school. Why, she and I can share a carriage out! I can see to it that she is safely settled!"

"Yes," the old man said dryly, "I suppose that is a most fortunate coincidence."

When Will was much smaller, he sometimes used to kneel at his great-uncle's feet, when he was in trouble or when he wanted something from him or when he was simply in need of some affection. I used to laugh at Will for this, saying that he looked no better than a well-trained puppy. In truth, I was jealous; jealous that he still had a relative in the world who would lay hands on his head with such obvious love.

Will's words of a few hours ago echoed in my ears as I entered the drawing room now, late in the evening before the morning of our departure. "Sure, I think you look fine in your suit," he'd said. "But remember: I am predisposed to think you look fine because you have dragged me along in your . . . *insanity.* But I do think that before you try your . . . *costume* out on the greater world, you should test it here at home first. After all, if you cannot fool one old man—and a blind one at that!—then how do you imagine you'll ever fool anyone else?" Here Will had heaved a heavy sigh. "Besides, Bet, I cannot bring myself to say goodbye to him, not under these circumstances. Who knows if I shall ever see him again? You be me for tonight."

An hour ago, I'd said goodbye to the old man as myself, wearing my wig and my usual dress. Our leave-taking had been a little formal, a little stiff, with me thanking the old man for everything he had done for me while he hemmed and hawed and asked if I needed anything else. But now, as I entered the drawing room in my suit and without the wig, for the first time I was Will Gardener.

"Who's that?" the old man said, cocking his head toward the doorway.

"It's me, Uncle," I said, hoping to God that I sounded enough like Will.

"Oh." He looked puzzled. "Your tread sounded slightly . . . *different* somehow."

Drat! I cursed my inability to exactly imitate Will's stride. But then I brightened. My tread might have sounded *slightly* off to the old man but clearly not off enough to make him immediately realize I was an impostor. Ever since I'd first come up with my plan, I'd behaved as though wholly convinced that I could succeed. I'd even told myself I could, repeatedly. In reality, all along there had been doubts plaguing me beneath the surface, fears that somehow I would be exposed before I even got the chance to start. But now I saw that those doubts had been unwarranted, and it was like the sun breaking through on a February day. Perhaps I really could pull this off!

I approached where the old man sat in his chair in front of the fire, taking care now to move with more of the hands-in-the-pockets casualness Will had taught me was the acceptable alternative to the other male form of walking, purposeful striding.

The old man cleared his throat. "When you and Elizabeth depart in the morning, I will still be in bed. Have you completed your packing yet?"

"Of course," I started, then, remembering that I was supposed to be Will—Will, who would never do anything now if he could do it later—I hastily added, *"not."*

The old man was silent for a moment, his mouth a round *o* of shock at Will's—*my*—insolence. And then he did a startling thing. He laughed.

"Oh, Will," he said, making a great effort to recover himself after his outburst of mirth, "in a strange way it is good to know that your unwillingness to toe the line is as reliable as death and taxes." He paused as a coughing fit overtook him. Then: "I suppose that you, being you, will not let the Betterman Academy get the better of you? And that after a fortnight or, at most, a whole term, you will arrange to have yourself sent down once more?"

A part of me understood that to successfully impersonate Will, I had to imitate what he would do in both word and deed. But another part of me, a part that was far stronger in that moment, could not allow the notion of myself as one who disappoints to continue—no matter who that self was supposed to be at the time.

I knelt at the old man's feet.

"You are wrong, Uncle," I vowed. "This time, things will be different. This time, I will distinguish myself."

He laughed once more. "Well, that should be easy enough."

"How do you mean?"

"Surely, you must have surmised by now that the Betterman Academy is a last ditch, a place where parents and guardians stow their charges when no one else in the world will have them; a place for misfits, miscreants, and ne'er-do-wells—you realize that, do you not?"

I felt my cheeks color at this, and when I spoke, it was with conviction. "Then it should be easy for me to distinguish myself, should it not? I shall be first among equals."

"You are serious, aren't you?" He was shocked; amazed, really.

"I am, sir. I mean, Uncle. What's more, I will write you every week to inform you of my progress. You will no doubt need something to occupy you, since I will be gone and that . . . *girl* will no longer be underfoot."

"I shall miss having the girl underfoot," the old man said softly, surprising me. "And, of course, I will miss you, boy."

And that's when he touched me. He placed his gnarled hand on my head like a benediction, and then, with great effort, he heaved himself forward enough in his chair so that he might kiss my brow.

"I love you, Will," he said gruffly.

"I love you too, Uncle," I responded clearly, not caring in the moment if Will would say that or not, only caring that the old man should hear those words from at least one of us, *someone,* before we left him behind.

Unlike Will, I had long since finished my packing. Indeed, I had been ready to go for days; the trunk Will had purchased for me was crammed full of the male clothing Will had given me, as well as one dress and my wig.

"You never know when you might need to be a girl again at a moment's notice" had been his mocking advice.

"And why would I need that?" I'd asked.

That's when he added details to my original plan. He said that in order to perpetuate the fiction that he was at school while I was companion to Mrs. Larwood, we'd need to arrange for things like visits home. Since Michaelmas half at the Betterman Academy ran from early September through the middle of December, I was to arrive home, as Will, in mid-December. Right before Christmas week, I, as Will, would announce that I was spending the holiday with a classmate's family. Then I would appear as myself, as the letter from Mrs. Larwood's daughter had indicated I would be given that week off. Once that week had passed, I would become Will again for the final week before returning to school. In this way, the old man would still be able to receive visits from both of us, even if he never saw us at the same time.

The machinations involved in what we were doing were enough to make my head spin!

I looked around the familiar bedroom, the room I had slept in for so long, the only such room I could remember clearly, my early childhood now being such a dim and distant dream. No one moved or spoke in the house around me, but I could not sleep, even though the only sound was the clock in the hallway ticking me toward morning and my new life. I lay with my head on the pillow.

Where would I lay my head the next night? I wondered. And where the night after that?

We departed in the still-dark hours of early morning. This worked well for our plan, since no one else in the house had yet risen. If they had been up, I would have had to put on a dress; the driver of the hired carriage would have been confused when I later changed and continued my journey as a young man. As it was, the man who drove us knew only that he had two young men to convey.

We left early so that we could reach our first destination, the inn where we would lodge at the halfway mark, by nightfall. As a result, I saw little. But then the sky began to lighten in minor increments as the horses clip-clopped their way along, and as we made our way out of the city, I began to catch glimpses of things I'd never seen before. It occurred to me then how small my world had been all my life. Why, I had never ventured any farther than church on Sundays! I had seen so little!

"What is that?" I would ask as we passed a particular building. "What kind of business do they do in there?"

"What is the name of this village?" I would ask. "Do you know what kind of work that farmer is doing?"

At first, Will was very patient in answering my many questions. But as the miles passed along with the hours, he grew somewhat less so. I realized this was because none of what we were seeing was new to him, but I didn't care.

"What?" he said. "Are you going to spend the whole day with your head hanging out the window, staring at *cows?*"

"Yes," I said. "Cows are new to me. It's *all* new to me."

"God," he said, not even bothering to hide his exasperation, "it's like traveling with a dog."

I took the briefest of moments to stick my tongue out at him before hanging my head back out the window.

"So what will the inn be like?" I asked with some excitement as the sky began to darken and we neared our first destination.

"Just like one cow is the same as the next, one inn is pretty much the same as the next." Will yawned. "There will be lots of wooden beams. There will be lots of fireplaces, but the fires will never be big enough to warm the rooms, and the lighting will be dim so you cannot see all the imperfections about you, or because the innkeeper is too cheap to spend more on oil, or perhaps both. There will be small bedrooms, with a bath down the hall, and a small dining room for taking meals. You will be glad then of the poor lighting because at least you won't have to see the wretched food."

The inn where we stopped for the night proved to be exactly as Will had predicted.

He registered us as Will Gardener and Will Smith.

"You were right that the room is small," I whispered to Will after we'd been shown up a narrow flight of stairs. "Now where is the second one?"

"The second what?"

"The second bedroom, of course," I said. "You know, one for me and one for you?"

"We are just getting the one room, Bet." Then he corrected himself. "Or I suppose I should say *Will.* After all, you will need to get used to answering to that name."

"Just one room?" I was shocked.

"Of course," he said, unpacking some items, "because one, it is cheaper, thereby leaving you with more spending money once you get to school; and two, you will need to get used to sharing a room with another boy."

"Another . . . ?"

"Of course," he said again. "What—did you think the Betterman Academy would treat you like a prince, granting you a room all to yourself?"

"You mean that at school I will be sleeping in the same room every night with *a boy?*"

"I take it you hadn't thought of that, then?"

If I hadn't been ready to faint at the prospect of what lay before me, I would have been tempted to slap that smile right off his face.

"Do not worry," Will said, removing one of the impossibly thin blankets from the bed and spreading it on the floor. "You can have the bed here. I suspect that I will have a few things to get used to myself and that once I am in the military there will be no comfy pillows for me. Now then." He clapped his hands together. "Dinner? I must say, I am *famished!*"

"You are not eating?" Will said, attacking his own meal with relish as we sat in the small dining room, the lighting turned so low one could barely see what one was eating.

"Mutton is not my favorite," I allowed.

"That is too bad, then." Will tore off a chunk of bread. "You will find that mutton is as omnipresent at school as cold water in the baths there . . . when there is water."

To say that I was growing increasingly nervous would be a gross understatement. And so, in order to disguise my nervousness, I bluffed like mad.

"That sounds wonderful!" I said brightly. "I am sure that I will find all of these challenges to be rather, um, character-building. No doubt it will make a man out of me!"

"You are an odd girl, Bet."

"I thought you were going to call me Will now," I countered.

"Very well, *Will.* You say you are ready for the challenges, but you have never been at school before. How do you propose to approach the actual *lessons?*"

"Lessons?"

"Yes, you know, that thing you are supposed to be there for—an education? You have never been in a classroom, have never taken any formal subjects in your life."

"Oh, that part will be easy," I said, and this time I wasn't bluffing. "Why, I can read anything, and I know a lot of history and literature, same as you. The difference is, I will work hard at those subjects and I will excel at them, since I will apply myself where you have not." I nervously twisted my napkin. "So, what other subjects will there be?"

"I would have thought you'd have asked about such things sooner, Bet, in terms of what to expect," Will said, eyeing my napkin-twisting. "You know, you can still change your mind . . ."

"Never," I said firmly, putting down the napkin with some force. "And stop calling me *Bet.*"

"What about mathematics, then? How is your Latin?"

"Does it matter?" I shrugged. "You have never done well at those subjects because they bore you." I shrugged again. "I could hardly do worse."

"You are maddening." He wiped his mouth hastily with his napkin before tossing it on the table and rising to his feet. "Come on. Let's go."

"Where are we going?" I wondered, rising just the same.

"To show you a little bit more of what you can expect at school."

Will took me hard by the elbow, steering me toward the door. "I don't know why I didn't think of this sooner."

❦

The night air was crisp as Will led me down the street. There were several small houses scattered along the way, a cheery light here, a welcoming wisp of smoke from a chimney there.

"Where are we going?" I demanded this time, seeking to extricate my elbow from Will's grasp, but he held firm.

"I will show you," he said. Then he muttered to himself, "Every small village has one. I should have been paying more attention as we rode in."

"One *what?*"

But Will wouldn't answer.

At last, we drew up to a squat building, the front of which had lots of small panes of glass, each pane its own small world shedding golden light outward onto the street. The door was open, and the sound of loud merrymaking poured out. I had never stood in front of a building such as this before, but I had read about these places in books.

"A *pub?* I can't go in there!"

I also knew from reading books that no lady—or at least, no lady who cared about her reputation—ever set foot in a pub.

"Of course you can," Will said, steering me toward the doorway. "You're Will Gardener now, aren't you? And this is the sort of thing Will Gardener does. It's what *all* boys who go off to school do: we squirrel away our money, and, whenever possible, we sneak out at night and go to the local pub to smoke and drink. Come on, then."

He yanked me through the door.

❦

"A pint of bitter for me, and a pint of ale for my friend here," Will ordered.

"I have never had a drink in my life," I said to him through gritted teeth as the publican moved to fill his order.

"No time like the present, then," Will said cheerfully, locating a small table for us. The table had a wobbly leg. Of course. "And you'll like the ale. It's easier than anything else to get used to. Much smoother. Why, you should be grateful I did not order you a whiskey first thing."

Will reached into his jacket and took out a small pouch from which he extracted a square of thin white paper and some flaky brown stuff. Then he put the brown stuff inside the paper and rolled it up.

"Smoke?" he offered.

"No, thank you," I said, waving the smoke away as he lit up. Not that my waving had any effect. The whole room was so filled with the stuff, it was like being in London on its foggiest day.

"Drink up," Will instructed when our drinks were delivered, taking a healthy draft from his own pint.

I was tempted to say "No, thank you" imperiously again, but then, thinking of what Will had said, that I would need to learn some of these things in order to fit in at school, I took a tentative sip.

"Huh," I said. "That's not bad." I had some more. "It's a lot drier than lemonade." I had some more. "In fact, since it's not sweet like lemonade, I can see where this could be very thirst-quenching on a hot day." I had—

"Slow down a bit." Will grabbed my wrist lightly. "You didn't really have any dinner. There's no need to drink the whole barrel your first night."

I hiccupped.

"Well, what do we have here?" I heard a female voice, a little rough sounding, say.

"Looks to me like two handsome young men out for a bit o' fun," a second female voice said, sounding even rougher than the first.

I looked up to see that two women had suddenly appeared to the right of our table. They looked to be not many years older than myself, but they wore paint on their faces; their lips somehow looked tired beneath the bright slashes of red. The low-cut bodices of their dresses were so tight, fleshy white breasts nearly spilled out from their tops. The one standing closer to Will was on the thin side, while the one beside me looked like she ate often.

"Buy a pair of pretty ladies drinks?" the one near Will said.

"Of course," he said with a smile. "Just go up and order whatever you want. My treat."

"What are you doing?" I demanded in a low voice as the women went off to the bar. "I thought you said that we, that *I,* would need as much money as possible for school."

Will shrugged and raised his glass. "A young man is always happy to buy a pretty lady a drink."

"But neither one of them is—"

"Here we are!" the thin one said. Then, without asking, she took a seat right in Will's lap. Before I knew what was happening, the heavier one was in mine.

"Such handsome young men," Will's new friend said, stroking his hair.

"They could be twins," mine added.

I was shocked that Will allowed himself to be stroked thus, shocked even more at my reaction at witnessing it. I wondered at my feelings, thought they might be jealousy. But then, through the fog of ale, I saw my feelings for what they were: I regarded Will as a sort of sibling, and seeing him like this now, I thought he was better than her. Or if not better than her, then better than this.

"Twins could be fun," Will's said.

"We've never had twins before," mine said. "What are your names?"

"I'm Will," Will said. "And, er, *he's* Will too."

"Oh," Will's said, looking mildly disappointed, "you're not twins, then." She shrugged, brightened. "Do you have a bit o' the ready?"

"What *are* they talking about?" I asked Will, not even bothering to modulate my tone now, as though the women weren't even there, as though no one could hear us and we existed in a universe of two.

"They are trying to ascertain," Will said, speaking clearly, "whether or not we have sufficient funds to obtain their services for the evening. You know, so we could bed them."

I was shocked. Will sounded so sure of himself. Had he bedded a woman before? And under similar circumstances? Then it hit me. Was this the sort of thing I would be expected to have knowledge of at school? And here I'd been amazed by *cows!*

"Haven't you ever been with a woman before, lad?" mine asked me. Not waiting for an answer, she thrust her hand between my legs and gave a hard squeeze. It was only later on that I realized that what she'd felt was the soft wadded-up ball of stocking I'd shoved down there. "No," she said, looking puzzled as her hand groped further, "I guess not."

"What are you *doing?*" I cried, abruptly rising from my seat and causing the woman to be dumped on the floor.

Will laughed uproariously at the sight.

"I'm sorry," he said to the women between gasping laughs, "I'm afraid we won't be needing your services this evening." Then he reached into his pocket and held out some coins to them with a good-natured shrug.

The one who'd been dumped on the floor looked angry at first, but then her friend started to laugh and finally she did too.

"At least we made some money," Will's said, helping her friend up, "and we didn't even have to do anything for it."

"What was that all about?" I asked Will once they were gone. "And what was that one woman expecting to find when she . . . *grabbed* me like that? I thought the stocking would be enough to fool anybody."

"Oh, Bet." Will shook his head at me, smiling a smile that was equal parts happy and sad. "I am worried about you."

"And why is that?"

"Because you really have no idea what you're getting yourself into, no idea how dangerous this game of yours might turn out to be."

"Dangerous?"

"I'm with you tonight, but after tomorrow morning I won't be. Anything could happen, and no one back home would even know where you were. Why, if the boys at school ever realize you're a girl, they'll eat you alive."

His words scared me. I can't say they didn't. But I'd already come so far.

"I'll take my chances," I said, then added, "Now order us another round."

A few hours later we stumbled our way back to the inn, arms flung around each other's shoulders. (The next day, as I continued my carriage ride alone, I would dimly recall that Will had taught me a song on the walk back, some strange song about a sailor.)

We further stumbled our way up the narrow flight of stairs and into our shared room, then collapsed onto our respective beds, still wearing our clothes. "You know, Bet," Will said drunkenly from his makeshift bed on the hard floor, "I've always regarded you as the sister I never had."

I was so stunned by this admission that it took me a long time to respond. I was unused to having someone express open affection for me in such a manner, and I wanted to return the favor, but it was awkward.

At last, I whispered, "I feel the same, Will. That is to say, I think of you as a brother, not a sister."

But by then it was too late, and my words were answered only with loud snores.

CHAPTER *five*

"Well, I am off to join the military," Will said brightly.

I squinched one eye open just wide enough to see him heft his bag. I'd been required to bring a large trunk to hold all the things I'd need at school, while Will had brought only a bag, since he said he wouldn't need very much where he was going. Even the single lamp he had lit gave off too much illumination, causing me to shut the eye again as quickly as I could. Thank God it was still too early for the morning sun.

"I am going to join the military," Will said again, more brightly yet.

"Yes, I heard you the first time," I murmured. "Before you go, do you think you might tell those people on the roof to stop pounding their hammers?"

"Poor Bet." Will laughed softly. Then I felt a feather kiss on my brow. "Good luck to you, sister."

"And you too, brother."

Then I rolled over and promptly fell back to sleep.

Later on I would count it a kindness that I had been too tired and too debilitated from the merrymaking of the night before to take proper note of Will's departure. Had I been fully aware of the reality—that we were parting now, and that I was to make the rest of my way alone—I might have begged him not to go.

Or at the very least, I might have begged him to take me with him.

❦

September 5, 18—

Dear Uncle,

Well, here I am at the Betterman Academy for Michaelmas half, and what a first three months this is going to be!

Although some may regard the Betterman Academy as "last ditch," I say it is grand! Did you know that Henry V commissioned it in 1414 as a charity school for poor boys? At the time, there weren't even seventy students here. I'll bet that old Henry never guessed that over four hundred years later, that number would swell to five hundred, with enough buildings to accommodate them! Of course, the students now are not poor.

And the buildings! All those spires! I'll bet old Henry didn't have so many spires himself at Windsor Castle! The chapel is an imposing structure, with all that stone and all those stained-glass windows and—you guessed it!—all those spires. The grounds are spectacular, and even the food here, which is served in Marchand Hall, is better than at any of the other fine educational institutions you sent me previously. Why, by the time I come home for Christmas, I think you will find me quite fat!

The master of the house where I am lodging, Proctor Hall, is named Mr. Winter. He is a kindly gentleman whom all the boys love. On my very first day here, he showed me around, arranged for my uniform—black tailcoat, waistcoat, false collar, white tie, and gray pinstriped trousers; only special students like school prefects and king's scholars are permitted to deviate from the uniform, wearing more colorful waistcoats—and introduced me to all.

I know you said that the students here would be—what was that phrase you used? Ah, yes. You said this was "a place for misfits, miscreants, and ne'er-do-wells." Well, I can personally assure you that that is not the case. Everyone I have met so far has been on best behavior, and I cannot imagine they are merely putting on a show for "the New Boy." Indeed, a finer group of young gentlemen I never expect to meet in life.

I have made several friends so far, including Hamish MacPherson, who is one of the school prefects and a real leader among the boys; Johnny Mercy, apparently Hamish's best friend and just as good as his name implies; Christopher "Little" Warren, who is called so because of his diminutive size and who is quite jolly about being nicknamed thus; and, of course, my roommate, James Tyler, who does not talk nearly so much as the others, remaining something of an enigma, but whom I think I shall grow to like.

Naturally, as much as I enjoy the company of the other boys here, I will not allow mere socializing to interfere with my studies. The Betterman Academy would appear to offer the finest educational opportunities, and I plan to pursue a course of . . .

I was sure—and I really was sure, since I had read all Will's letters to his great-uncle—that Will had never written such an exclamatory letter in his life. Still, I wanted the old man to have some joy, to believe that this time things would be different, better. Nonetheless, even I could stomach the telling of only so many lies. For what in my entire letter had been the truth? The architectural descriptions, surely, but little else. I therefore finished with a loving signature and sealed up the letter after also including a second letter from Bet, having contrived a postscript explaining that Bet was including her letters to Uncle whenever she wrote to Will so that Will could forward them for her and Bet could save on postage. And I had come up with *that* contrivance so I would not have to create a false address from which to send Bet's letters.

Oh, my head was starting to spin! What a tangled web I was weaving now that I practiced to deceiving!

❦

God, it was noisy in this place! How loud the world had grown, and how many people were in it!

Mr. Winter, the master of Proctor Hall, was a short man, round as a Christmas goose, with little hair, only a horseshoe of black rimming his otherwise bald pate. He was also, apparently, a deaf man, for he did not seem to notice the overabundance of noise that thundered the walls as he led me up the stairs to my room.

As we turned onto the landing, with me barely able to drag the heavy trunk up the stairs behind me, I caught my first sight of three of my floor mates. One was a tall hulk of a boy with yellow hair and disturbingly pale blue eyes. He had on a purple and red waistcoat, a sign that he was somehow different from the rest of us. Another one of the boys was also tall, but he had the build of a twisted string bean, and his brown hair and squinty brown eyes gave him the appearance of a rodent. As for the third boy, who had a shock of curly red hair badly in need of cutting, it was difficult to gauge his height since he was curled up in the large arms of the first boy.

"Ooh, New Boy," the hulking one said upon seeing me. I couldn't be entirely positive, but I was fairly certain that that was a sneer I saw stretching out his lips. Then, as though my arrival were of no immediate importance, he turned his attention back to the string bean. "Here, catch," he said.

Before I knew what was happening, the hulking one tossed the boy he was holding, and the string bean stretched out his arms, just barely grasping and holding on to the flying object.

Mr. Winter began to lead us past as though nothing out of the ordinary were happening.

"Your turn," the string bean said, and suddenly the third boy was flying through the air again, only this time he was screaming.

I couldn't believe what I was seeing: they were playing catch with a human being!

"Um, shouldn't someone do something about that?" I suggested to Mr. Winter, casting furtive glances over my shoulder as the master plodded down the hall.

"Whatever for?" he said. "It's just high spirits."

"Yes, but someone could get"—I heard a loud thump behind me, the third boy crashing to the floor—"hurt."

"Pish-tosh. Boys will, after all, be boys." He stopped in front of a closed door. "Here we are."

Mr. Winter turned the knob without knocking first.

Later on, I would more fully register the appearance of the room that was to be my home for however long I could get away with my plan: the lone narrow window that let in little light even at high noon; the fireplace with no logs in it; the hardwood floors with no carpet to warm one's feet on cold mornings; the walls that perhaps had once been cream but were now stained to more of a grayish brown in spots; the two wooden desks and chairs, more utilitarian than decorative, as were the two wardrobes; the two narrow beds, shoved up against opposite walls.

I would take in all of the meagerness of my new lodgings later, because in that moment I was too busy taking in the first sight of the person I would be sharing it with.

"Gardener, meet James Tyler," Mr. Winter said, introducing us, although I must confess, I barely registered the words.

I'd read about beauty in books. I'd even seen some of it in the world. But I'd never before seen so much of it gathered up into a single human being.

James Tyler was a good six inches taller than me; lean without being skinny; with hair that looked like a successful alchemist had fashioned it, adding just a hint of platinum to all that gold; and eyes the color of the ever-changing sea.

"Pleased to meet you," he said, holding out a hand with fingers so long and strong, I thought he must be able to play piano concertos.

I know I must have stammered out something, but later on I could not for the life of me remember what that something had been. I do know it was a long moment before I had the presence of mind to thrust out my own hand and feel the warmth of his fingers as he grasped it.

"You should be safe enough, at least while you are in here," Mr. Winter said, clapping his hand on my shoulder briefly, preparatory to his departure. "Tyler is one of our more, er, *human* students." He left the room.

"Shall I show you around?" my new roommate offered.

"I wish you would," I said, only belatedly remembering that it was high time I let go of his hand. I prepared to follow him wherever he might lead, anywhere.

"Wouldn't you like to stow your things first?"

"Hmm?" I was still dwelling on the warmth of those fingers touching mine.

"Your things." He indicated the trunk behind me.

"Oh!" I said, surprised to see the handle still in my hand; I looked at the trunk as though it were a persistent stranger who had followed me in.

"I've already put mine in the wardrobe on the right," he said helpfully.

Glancing over, I saw that he'd left the wardrobe slightly ajar, and I observed all manner of masculine clothing peeking out. That casualness certainly wouldn't do for me, not when in addition to the suits and other articles I'd packed there was also a dress and wig.

Opening the wardrobe on the left, I inquired, casually, I hoped, "Are there, um, keys for these wardrobes?"

"Should be one on the top," James said, reaching over my head and, sure enough, producing a dusty key.

"Thank you." I deposited the trunk hastily in the bottom of the wardrobe, turned the key in the outer lock, twisted the handle to make sure the door was secure, and pocketed the key.

"You don't need to do that around here," James said, giving me an odd look. "No one will steal your suits."

"Well"—I forced a cheery smile—"with boys being boys, one never knows, does one?" Before he could say anything else, I added, "I'm ready for that tour now!"

❦

I may have been overwhelmed by the beauty of James Tyler initially, but I got over it just as quickly when we exited our room and I caught sight of the same three boys I'd seen earlier. Funny how quickly violence can make one forget all about beauty.

James hurried us toward the game of human catch, seemingly as oblivious to what was happening as Mr. Winter had been.

"Tyler," the hulking one said with a curt nod before tossing the boy ball to the string bean once again.

"MacPherson." My roommate returned the nod, curtness and all, as we passed.

"Looks like New Boy's almost as delicate as Little here," the one my roommate had referred to as MacPherson said. "It's amazing the trouble he had carrying his own trunk. I'll bet New Boy'd make a fine new ball for us."

The string bean snickered.

"I wouldn't try it if I were you," my roommate said cheerfully enough, not even bothering to turn around as he led me briskly back down the stairs.

❦

As James showed me around the grounds that afternoon, he spoke very little other than to name the buildings he pointed out and sometimes add a sentence about what each was for. He was neither friendly nor specifically unfriendly; he was merely there.

Walking past the school gates with the oriel window soaring above, traversing the gravel walk to the side of the commons, I got the sense he was leading me on the tour more because he felt it was his duty rather than because he took any joy in my company. Indeed, something about him said that he almost always preferred being alone to being with others. Still, I was grateful at least to have someone to walk with—already I sensed that it could get lonely for me here at the Betterman Academy—and I sought to enliven our walk with a little conversation.

"Those three back there," I said, with a nod at Proctor Hall. "Who are they?"

"The large blond one is Hamish MacPherson, Proctor Hall's school prefect. The tall thin one is Johnny Mercy."

"And the one they were, er, throwing?"

"Christopher Warren. Everyone calls him Little. He hates it."

"Except for that last bit," I said, trying on a laugh, "it doesn't really tell me much about them, does it?"

He stopped walking to look at me. "Didn't what you saw back there tell you everything you need to know?" he said evenly. Then he started walking again. "Besides, you'll see plenty more at dinner."

At dinnertime Marchand Hall rang with the sound of five hundred chairs scraping the hardwood floor as seats were pulled out, five hundred plates hitting the tables, five hundred glasses being set down, five hundred sets of silverware clinking as five hundred linen napkins were unrolled. Marchand Hall also rang with the sounds of, as Mr. Winter would have it, boys being boys.

James and I sat side by side at a long table with Mr. Winter at one end and Hamish MacPherson at the other. I would have liked to sit almost anywhere else, but according to James it was the custom at the Betterman Academy for boys to sit at tables with their floor mates.

"I keep telling you," Hamish said, addressing Johnny Mercy, "that the idea is to *catch* Little, not *drop* him."

Little, I noted, was now sporting a large bandage over his right eye.

"I would never have *dropped* him," Mercy returned, "if you could learn how to *throw* him."

"Don't you two ever get tired of this game?" James said, sounding bored.

I wanted to say I agreed with him—it seemed to me that this game they played did get tiresome quickly—but the scowl Hamish shot in James's direction was enough to keep my mouth shut.

"Always think you're better than everyone else, don't you, Tyler?" Hamish said.

To this, James gave no answer. I think it was because the answer was too obvious: James *was* better than everyone else. At least, he was better than Hamish.

Hoping not to be noticed, I looked down at the plate that had been set before me. The small piece of meat on it was . . . *mysterious;* mysterious and, I suppose, *stringy* would be the next appropriate word.

Still, I was suddenly famished, not having had anything to eat since the meager breakfast I'd barely been able to consume at the inn that morning, so many hours ago now; my stomach at the time had been shaky after Will's and my adventures of the night before.

I took up knife and fork, preparing to tuck in.

"Don't you know anything, Gardener?" Hamish said.

So caught up was I in my own hunger, I didn't really register the words as I attempted to cut the meat.

"Hey! Gardener! I'm talking to you!"

I felt something bounce against my forehead and looked up in time to see that it was a dinner roll.

I realized then that I was going to have to start being more careful, pay closer attention. Hamish had somehow learned my name and had been addressing me, but I'd ignored him because I still wasn't used to my own name!

Hoping to speak as little as possible—for in my hungry and tired state, I feared that I'd forget to speak like a boy—I simply looked at Hamish, the question in my eyes.

"We wait for grace around here before we eat," Hamish informed me, causing me to drop my knife and fork as though they were hot coals when I realized my error. "Don't you know anything?"

The room fell silent, as if on cue, as Reverend Parkhurst, standing at the head of the room, waited for us all to rise before saying grace over the meal.

"*Now* you can eat," Hamish told me when the reverend had finished and five hundred chairs had been pulled out again, five hundred boys had sat down.

I took up knife and fork once more.

"My *God,*" Hamish said. "You're worse than Little here. One would think you'd never been at school before. This your first time away from *Mummy?*"

Much as I wanted to keep silent, I couldn't stop myself from speaking up.

"My mother is dead," I said, straightening my spine as I spoke the truth for both Will and myself.

"Yeah, well, whose isn't? I'll still bet anything this is your first time away at school."

"Actually, it is my fifth," I said, adopting Will's biography with no small degree of pride.

I felt James's eyes boring into me from the side, but I kept my eyes steadily on Hamish.

"Your *fifth?*" His eyebrows rose up nearly to his hairline. "Why, even Mercy and me've only been at three, including here." He waved his fork at me. "What sorts of things were you sent down for?"

I studied the ceiling, hoping to get the order right.

"Let's see . . . cheating, lying . . . no, that's the wrong order. Lying, cheating, general mischief, and setting the headmaster's house on fire."

Hamish stared at me. They all did. Then Hamish threw back his head and roared.

"Well, at least you've got the lying part right," he said. "I've never heard anything more ridiculous in my life."

"Ridiculous?"

"Yes, ridiculous. Who'd ever believe someone like you capable of all that?"

All right, so maybe I had appropriated someone else's record as my own, but Will Gardener *had* done all those things, and I felt unaccountably offended at this accusation.

"If you don't believe me," I said, showing more steel than I knew I had, "then why don't you have Mr. Winter look into my history?"

Hamish stared at me so long and hard, I thought my own eyes would fall out from the effort of staring back just as long, just as hard.

"Never mind," he said, his gaze dropping before mine did. "No need to embarrass you by catching you out in a lie. I will say one thing, though."

"And that is?" I asked.

"You've got spirit."

Little leaned across the table, and I heard him speak for the first time, in a voice that squeaked. "Hamish hates people with spirit," he whispered helpfully.

As soon as dinner ended, Hamish asked with an inscrutable smile if James and I would like to join him and some of the others for a stroll. I confess that, given what had gone before, I was more than a little startled at this overture of friendship. But figuring that it would not do to look the proverbial gift horse in the mouth and not wanting to make an enemy of him, or more of an enemy than he already appeared to be, I opened my mouth to accept. Perhaps he wanted to start fresh?

That's when my roommate, almost silent throughout dinner, spoke up to decline. For both of us.

"Thank you for the kind offer, MacPherson," he said evenly. "But I'm afraid Gardener and I already have plans."

Hamish's eyebrows shot up at this, as did my own.

We had plans?

"Fine," Hamish said at last, smiling as though not bothered in the slightest although the tightness of that smile and the firm set of his jaw said otherwise. "Suit yourselves."

"We have plans?" I asked James, having followed him out of the dining hall and practically scampering to keep up as he strode briskly across the commons toward Proctor Hall.

"Yes," he said, his tone matching his stride. "We have plans *not* to get caught up in any of MacPherson's idiocy on our first night here."

"Oh." I hadn't imagined that there was going to be any idiocy. But now I was curious. "What sort of idiocy will there be?"

"They will drink. They will smoke."

"But isn't that what everyone does here?" I asked, remembering what Will had told me of school. "Why, I drink and smoke all the time," I bluffed. "Don't you do those things?"

He stopped walking, eyed me with disbelief. "Sometimes," he finally allowed. "But when MacPherson and Mercy do it, someone always gets hurt. Usually it's Little who winds up with his head shoved in the privy hole down by the playing fields. But since it's your first night here and MacPherson has already warmed to you so much"—he barked a bitter laugh at this—"I thought this time they might choose to pick on *you* instead. Is that what you want?"

I shook my head, although I doubted he could see the vehemence of that headshake in the gloom of the gathering night.

"No, I didn't think so," he said, as though he had seen me. "Besides which, you seem like a good sort"—he paused, then added—"even if you don't appear to know what to do half the time."

"What does that mean?" I demanded.

"Back there." He indicated Marchand Hall. "You were about to accept Hamish's invitation, weren't you?"

"Well, y-yes," I stammered. "I thought perhaps he wanted to start fresh."

"Start fresh?" He laughed. "People like Hamish and Johnny don't *start fresh*. You do realize, don't you, that they are bullies?"

I must confess that, while I'd recognized them as being somewhat cruel, I hadn't thought about them as actual bullies. Bullies were the sort of thing I'd only read about.

"Are you scared of MacPherson?" I asked. It seemed a sensible enough question to me. Already, based on personal observation and experience, not to mention what James had just said, I was scared of MacPherson.

"Don't be daft." James laughed. "But only a fool seeks out trouble if he can possibly avoid it."

"And how should one behave around here if one wishes to avoid trouble?" I asked. Seeing the skeptical look on his face, I hastened to add, "I only ask in case it's different here than at the four other schools I've been to. My uncle will murder me if I get sent down again."

"The usual." He shrugged. "Don't talk about home, or you'll be made fun of for being homesick. Answer questions straightforwardly, hold your head up, and you'll get on."

"Sounds easy enough." I sighed my relief.

"Oh, and one other thing."

"Hmm?"

"Be sure there's nothing odd about you."

Back in our room, we passed the next few hours in companionable silence. James removed his tailcoat and tie and loosened his collar, then lay on his stomach across one of the beds, reading a book. I tried to make out the title but couldn't read it from my own position in one of the stiff chairs before one of the utilitarian desks. If anyone had asked what I was reading that night, I could not have said. My mind was too many things at once: exhausted by all that had happened since I'd left Grangefield Hall, just yesterday morning; nervous at the prospect of all the new things that were yet to come. So rather than actually read what was in front of me, I simply stared at the words, my fingers turning pages for no reason as my mind raced and stalled, stalled and raced.

It was coming on eleven when James tossed his book to one side and gave a great, heaving yawn.

"I think I will turn in," he said, the first words either of us had spoken in about three hours. "First day of classes tomorrow and I should like to be well rested for it. I suggest you do the same."

Then he walked over to the twin basins that were kept in the room for convenience sake, washed his face with water from the first, and cleaned his teeth with water from the second.

I suppose if I had not been so utterly exhausted by that point, I would have guessed what was coming next. But I was exhausted, and I had not guessed.

Obviously without a thought in the world, James began removing his clothing.

Too stunned to do anything else, I stared as article after article was shed until finally he stood there as God had made him. I thanked that same God that James was not paying any attention to me and thus did not catch me staring.

Prior to this, I had seen many pictures in art books of naked people. But even Michelangelo had had only paints and stone to work with. This was a living and breathing boy, muscle and sinew and flesh. He was naked, and, I blush to confess, he was magnificent.

Thankfully, before I could do something truly foolish—like reaching out to touch that skin to see if it felt as marvelous as it looked—James slipped a nightshirt over his head and climbed into his bed.

"Are you going to stay up?" he asked, casting a meaningful look at the lamp on my desk.

"Of course not." I blushed again.

I too went to the basin and washed my face and teeth as he had done, then I unlocked the wardrobe and removed from my trunk the nightshirt Will had loaned me.

My mind had been exhausted just a short time ago, but it was fully awake now.

So many things I hadn't thought about before! So many things I hadn't planned on!

I crossed the room to open the narrow window. It took some doing, for the window was jammed.

"What are you doing?" James inquired, leaning up on one elbow. "Are you one of these sorts who need fresh air to sleep?"

"No," I said. Having at last forced open the window, I reached out and pulled the outer shutters in so tight that not even the merest sliver of moonlight could penetrate into the room. "I'm one of these sorts who need total darkness to sleep."

I shut the window, extinguished the lamp. Only when the room was pitch-black did I commence removing my own clothes, intensely aware with every button I undid that I had never been naked in front of anyone in my life, unless one counted when one was a baby, which I did not, and this first person I was naked in front of was a boy.

Thank God he could not see me.

I hurried out of the rest of my day clothes, hurried into my nightshirt, and practically dove between the sheets of my bed. Unfortunately, not being able to see anything, I barked my shin against the bedpost.

"Ouch," James said in the darkness.

"Yes," I agreed, wincing.

"Shall I plan on you doing this routine every night?" James wondered.

"Hopefully I won't bark my shin every night." I blushed in the dark before admitting, "But yes, pretty much."

"Modest?" he inquired.

"Hideous scar," I replied, praying he would accept that. "I don't like to make other people scream at the sight of it if I can help it."

"It can't be all that bad," he said.

"You have no idea."

"Very well then. I suppose, when I remember, I can wait out in the hall and let you change first. That should save your shins a bit."

I was startled at this kindness.

"Thank you," I said simply.

I heard him yawn again.

"You are an odd one, aren't you, Will?" Despite his words, which were less a question than a statement, and despite what he'd said earlier about how "odd" was to be avoided if one wanted to stay out of trouble, I heard no rancor. He was merely making an observation. And I did like that he, unlike Hamish and the others, used my given name, at least when we were alone together.

"James," I said, using his name for the first time, enjoying the feel of the letters forming in my mouth, before I repeated the words I'd spoken just a moment ago, "you have no idea."

CHAPTER *six*

September 10, 18—

Dear Bet,

Well, I have done it! I am now officially a servant in Her Majesty's military! And I owe it all to you. You know, when you first came up with what I've always referred to as your harebrained scheme, I thought you were mad and said as much. But I don't think I have ever said—and now find that I must, now that I have at least embarked on the achievement of my life's ambition—how damned grateful I am to you for that harebrained scheme. After all, were it not for you, I would not be here.

And where exactly is here? You may well ask. "Here" is with others of my kind, young men who, for whatever reason, wish to give their lives to military service.

You will laugh to hear this, but enlisting was just as easy as I told you it would be. After leaving you at the inn early that morning, I made my way to the next town over, and, before the sun had even risen very high in the sky, I glimpsed a man setting up a stall right in the street, seeking fresh recruits. He did not ask my age, but having visually assessed me and decided I was "on the youngish side," he gave me a special appointment.

I am to be a drummer boy! Now, do not keep laughing, for I am certain that once I have been with the regiment for enough time and had the chance to prove myself, I will be given even greater opportunities to show my value. In the meantime, I will just pound, pound, pound away on my drum for all I am worth. You know I have never played an instrument before, save for a few notes on the piano, but I am finding the drum to be rather easy to master. If one just pounds loudly and at regular intervals, others seem to be pleased enough with the efforts.

I am also finding the men I serve with to be a most capital group of fellows—honestly, they are better in every way than anyone I ever knew at school. And the food! People will say that military food is the worst, but let me assure you, it is not half bad! My sleeping accommodations, in case you are worried about me, are also quite adequate. Really, I don't know why people fuss so about the hardships of the military, for I feel as though I am living like a prince!

I write to you before we ship out. Curiously enough, I do not know yet where my ultimate destination will be, only that we are leaving soon. When I asked an older gentleman in my regiment where we might be going, he said that it could be almost anywhere, and he provided me with a long list of possibilities: the North-West Frontier, Burma, Abyssinia—really, he said we might wind up anywhere! When I inadvertently expressed some mild shock—for some reason, I had expected that everyone who joined up all went to one place—the older gentleman laughed and said, "It isn't easy running the world, you know!"

So, not knowing where I will soon be departing for, not knowing what sort of night sky I will be gazing up at a month from now—it is all an adventure to me!

Please do write back, to the general address I will provide below. I am told that it sometimes takes the post a long time to catch up with men in the service, but eventually it does find us!

And please do not worry in the slightest. I am healthy and well fed and, most of all, happy. And I owe it all to you.

Your brother in spirit,
Will

"Is something wrong?" James's voice startled me.

"I'm sorry, what are you talking about?" I'd been so caught up in reading Will's words, I had not heard James come in. Now I hurried to put the letter in my desk, fearing he would see that damning salutation at the top of the page: *Dear Bet.*

"It's just that . . ." Here James gestured to the corners of his eyes, as though I were a deaf person and he was seeking to make me understand. Then he further explained, "You look as though you have been crying."

It was only then that I realized that tears had sprung to my eyes as I had read Will's letter. The cause? Did I need just one? I missed him dreadfully, because he truly was my brother in spirit and I felt so alone where I was now. I missed him because I was often confused by the new life I was living and he was no longer here to help guide me. And yet I was glad for him, because obviously he had found happiness.

"Oh, no," I said, brushing the tears abruptly from my cheeks. "It is just all the dust in here." I waved my hand around the room. "I have always been bothered by dust."

James looked around pointedly. In fact, our room was spotless, kept so by our zealous matron and housekeeper, Mrs. Smithers. Mrs. Smithers was responsible for, among other things, arranging our tea, seeing to it that our boots and shoes were polished and left at the ready beneath our beds, and ensuring that fresh linens were regularly distributed. Except for the tops of the wardrobes, which she could not reach, she dusted everywhere; she had a passion for dusting that bordered on obsession. A pleasant enough woman, she did take the execution of her duties to extremes.

"Then there's nothing wrong at home?" James prompted.

"Why should there be anything wrong at home?"

"You were reading a letter, and you did look"—he paused, perhaps reluctant to accuse me of crying again—"*something*. And most letters do come from home, so I simply assumed . . ."

Now I understood. Wanting to correct his misapprehension, and perhaps in part because I was so proud of Will, I enthusiastically explained the situation to him.

"Not at all!" I said. "The letter was from a friend who recently entered into military service!"

"Capital!" James said, matching my own enthusiasm as he took a seat on the edge of his bed. "I have always wondered what military life was actually like."

I proceeded to tell him some of the highlights from Will's letter, omitting of course what Will's true relationship to me was, and not mentioning the fact that *he* was the real Will Gardener that James was supposed to be sharing his room with.

But as I prattled cheerily on, James's face, which had been so eager when I first started talking, began to fall.

"What is the matter?" I finally asked with no small exasperation, grinding my chipper narrative to a halt.

"Only that your friend is telling you a pack of lies," he said with a rare blush.

"What?" I was outraged.

"Oh, I believe the part about him being made a drummer—that is the sort of menial job the military would give to a young man with no experience. But the rest? All that about the wonderful food and the good accommodations and all the fellows being just capital? Lies. All of it."

I had never understood before why boys got into physical scrapes with one another, prompted to fisticuffs by some offense, real or imagined. But I certainly understood it now. I wanted to throttle James. For the implied aspersion on Will's character. For the smug look on his face.

But before I could react, either with my fists or with words, James went on.

"I have read many accounts of life in the military, and nothing your friend says, save that part about being a drummer, rings true."

I saw it then: the truth in what he was saying. Writing to Paul Gardener as Will, I myself had told a pack of lies about how things were at the Betterman Academy. I had told those lies because I did not want to hurt him, did not want him to worry. Why, then, should it be so surprising that Will would treat me the same way? It made me wonder what the true state of affairs was for Will in his new life.

Still, realizing that Will had lied while James had told the truth did not make me any less angry with James. When kings received bad news, they rarely directed their immediate displeasure at the source, which might be miles or even countries away; instead, they unleashed their wrath upon the bearers of the tidings.

"Well!" I said heatedly. I decided that my initial good impression of James, my sense that he was someone I would like to be friends with—all right, I had also found him intensely attractive—had been false. Upon better acquaintance I concluded that I did not like him half so much as I'd thought. "You did say you wondered what military life was actually like. And now that I have given you one such account, you tell me about contrary accounts you have read in *books!*" I never would have guessed that I, who loved books so much, could invest so much contempt in the word *books.* "So, perhaps, it is your *books* that are lying!"

At first, James just sat there, stunned. Then a look of exasperation came over his face. Perhaps upon better acquaintance, he had concluded that he did not like me half so much either? Perhaps he no longer wished to be friends?

I immediately regretted my hasty words. For if I didn't have James for a friend here, who would I have? It was a frightening thought, the idea of being that alone.

I had always hated swallowing my pride, yet I did so now.

But as I opened my mouth to say something conciliatory, James stormed from the room.

There was so much for me to acclimate myself to at the Betterman Academy, I had precious little time to spare for lesser things, like, say, the annoyances of roommates. Roommates who were annoying because they could become as unreasonably exasperated as, say, I could.

For one thing—all right, two—there were Latin and Greek. I had had little experience with either, but thankfully, many of my classmates seemed to find them one big mystery as well. We each struggled independently with our own individual vulgus, English paragraphs that we were supposed to translate into Latin. Homer's *Iliad,* Homer's *Odyssey*—the two works might have been interchangeable as far as most students were concerned, since to those same students, the epics were merely words to be translated back and forth, as though all of education could be reduced to rote learning. Livy, Virgil, Euripides—to the other students, they were just unpleasant, often confusing jobs to be finished.

I must confess that I attacked these tasks with more eagerness than most of my classmates, earning me no small amount of criticism from Hamish and Mercy. They seemed to find it particularly worthy of comment when, in a different lesson, one touching on the works of Shakespeare, I showed a marked interest in *Twelfth Night,* the play about a young woman named Viola who masquerades as a young man when circumstances dictate.

"Perhaps Gardener would like to masquerade as a young woman," Hamish said with a sneer from somewhere behind me.

"Oh, Gardener already seems something of a young woman to me," I heard Mercy respond. Mercy, in his endless attempts to ingratiate himself with Hamish, constantly tried to improve upon Hamish's insults to others. Sometimes, and in this instance thankfully for me, since it provided a needed distraction, Hamish would instead grow annoyed with Mercy, as though he feared that Mercy was seeking to wrest primacy from him.

As they began to fight between themselves, I gave a sigh of relief, even as I noted that seemingly innocent things on my part—like showing an interest in a play about mistaken identity—could be a source of problems.

And there was no shortage of problems for me at the Betterman Academy.

Take, for instance, singing.

We had academic lessons five days a week and half a day on Saturday. This meant that by the time Saturday night came, the boys were eager for entertainment, and entertainment, at least at the Betterman Academy, meant singing. From the hidden bottled-beer cellar that Mercy kept stocked—one of his chief values to Hamish, I quickly learned, along with the hampers of wine and game Mercy frequently received from home—beer would be smuggled in as, one after another, we took turns exhibiting our vocal talents. In front of the fireplaces in the great room at the bottom of Proctor Hall, mugs were knocked together in toasts and much hand-shaking went on following the better performances. The problem was that everyone was expected to perform, and, despite my talent for imitating speaking voices, I could not sing to save my life.

"Oh, Gardener!" Hamish covered his ears. "Please stop that infernal racket! You sound like a regular Jenny."

I had learned that when someone wanted to make particular fun of a boy, he would call him by a girl's name, as though being a girl were the worst thing possible.

"Don't we have penalties for people who sing poorly?" Mercy suggested, placing a thoughtful finger to his lower lip.

In a minute, he was trailing behind Hamish as the two raced from the room.

"You might want to run for it now, before they get the blanket," one of the younger boys advised me.

"There's no point in him running," Little said resignedly, as though I weren't even there. "They always catch a person."

Little was right. Before I'd realized that I might be in danger for the crime of being a poor singer, Hamish and Mercy had returned.

And that's when I learned all about tossing, which is exactly what it sounds like: they put a person in a blanket and then they toss the person. I also learned quickly that it only hurts the person when he or she is dropped, and, further, that the ones doing the tossing get really mad if the one being tossed refuses to kick and struggle and scream. I refused to do any of those things, and so by the time Hamish and Mercy were done with me and I'd survived my first tossing, they clearly hated me even more than when they'd put me in the blanket.

And where was my roommate, James, through all of this?

Why, he was in our room, of course.

For that was one other thing I'd learned in my short time at the Betterman Academy: the rules that applied to the rest of us—like compulsory singing on Saturday nights and, in the case of younger or new students such as myself, remaining in the corridors for long hours on alternating nights in case a more senior boy wanted something—didn't apply to James.

Two weeks into my stay at the Betterman Academy, disaster struck.

I should have anticipated it, and yet I had not: there was blood on my sheets.

After my first night at school, when I'd realized that boys commonly dressed and undressed in front of one another, I'd trained myself to rise early enough so that James was still asleep, moving about the room as noiselessly as possible while hurrying into my clothes so he'd never catch a glimpse of what I looked like without them.

But on that morning I realized that my usual strategy was futile. One look at my sheets—and he would surely see them, for it would be supremely odd for any Betterman boy to make his own bed, a task always left for the housekeeper—and I'd be exposed. It was challenge enough getting dressed before he arose, especially having to bind my breasts, which I let spring free at night once I was sure he was asleep; the morning's added challenge of having to find suitable cloths with which to stanch the flow made the whole an impossibility.

As I lay there, feeling the familiar dull ache in my lower abdomen and cursing myself—how could I not have foreseen *this?*—I heard him stir.

I looked over to see him propping himself up on his elbows and emitting a large early-morning yawn.

"Well, here's a novelty," he observed. "You usually get up so much before me that I'd grown to believe either you sleep in your clothes or you never sleep at all. Is something wrong?"

Oh, the understatement!

"I'm not feeling well today," I said, sheets and blankets pulled up tight under my chin so he could see nothing. "I think I may need to skip first lesson."

"Skip first lesson?" he echoed. "Almost no one ever does that. Old Man Peters won't be happy."

"Old Man Peters is so old, I doubt he'll even notice one less student," I quipped.

"I suppose," he conceded, rising and stripping off his nightshirt as he did so.

Every time he did that, it was as though he were doing it for the first time, and I had to force my eyes away from the sight of him naked.

"What do you think it is," he said as he stood before a basin, still maddeningly naked, washing his face, "this thing that has you feeling not well?"

"Did you eat the meat at dinner?" was my rejoinder.

"It is sometimes best avoided," he admitted ruefully, pulling out fresh clothes.

He proceeded to don them at such a leisurely rate, I was tempted to scream, *Oh, will you just get on with it and get out of here?* But of course I couldn't do that.

"Can I get you something before I go?" he asked, at last tying his tie. Thank *God!* "Perhaps some plain toast or a cup of tea? I could ask Mrs. Smithers—"

"I'll be fine," I snapped, cutting him off. "Really, by second lesson, I'll be right as rain."

He studied me for a moment, as though I were a curiosity.

"Huh," he said finally. "It must be a wonderful thing, knowing the exact moment one will be well again."

As soon as the door shut behind him and I heard his booted feet head down the corridor, I sprang out of bed and immediately locked the door.

Turning around, I saw the damning red stains on my sheets, but I couldn't do anything about that just yet. First, I needed to stanch the bleeding.

My nightshirt was a dead loss, I saw as I whipped it off; I rolled it into a ball and tossed it to one side. Then I sought out the stack of washing cloths that Mrs. Smithers left along with our fresh linens every day. I selected one that looked to be about the right size and thickness.

Back at Grangefield Hall a year ago, when I'd experienced my first bleeding, it was one of the maids, Sara, who'd done what my mother would have done had she still been alive: explained to me the regularity of the monthly flow, how it related to the making of babies, and what to do about the bleeding. She'd given me special pieces of cotton fabric, about two feet by one foot in measure, the central foot or so composed of a thicker terry-cloth material. Sara had folded it into thirds and shown me how to wear it.

Of course, no specially designed pieces of cloth would be available to me here unless I stole them from Mrs. Smithers's rooms—and such a theft might look suspicious—so I had to make do as best I could with what was available.

Once that was in place, I dressed quickly, collected the sheets, and made straight for Mrs. Smithers's rooms, feeling it best to deal with her as directly as possible while recognizing that in the future I'd need to anticipate my monthly flow so as not to repeat the occurrence.

Mrs. Smithers was about forty years of age and rotund (she didn't seem to mind the food that most of us hated); her graying hair poked out from under her bonnet.

She eyed me suspiciously as I explained about the sheets.

"Impetigo," I said with a nervous laugh, naming a disease I'd read about. "It causes unpredictable bleeding sometimes, but it can also be a bit contagious." Another nervous laugh. "So you might just want to burn those."

"Will this be happening often?"

"Oh, no!" I reassured her.

"But I thought you just said it was unpredictable?"

"Yes, well, but I have been getting a lot better in recent years. You should have seen me when I was just a little tyke!" I held out my hand, illustrating the height of this imaginary little tyke. "I used to bleed like a geyser regularly! But now?" I shrugged. "Almost nothing."

The way Mrs. Smithers was eyeing me, I realized I was talking too much, too fast.

"Yes, well . . . sorry to have been a bother! Thank you!" I said, rushing from her presence.

Back in my own room, I grabbed the soiled nightshirt and hid it beneath my jacket; the location of the bloodstain on it might have been too suspicious if I'd given it with the sheets to Mrs. Smithers. Outside, I hurried to the wooded area behind one of the less-used playing fields and scrabbled in the dirt until the evidence was buried. It was only then that it occurred to me that once a month I would need to find a way to steal several cloths from Mrs. Smithers's supply, and all of those would need to be buried out here as well. And then of course I would need to find excuses to explain to James why sometimes the supply was short. Perhaps I would need to invent a strong wine habit for her?

It was so much to think about, so much to do—and to address one little item!

One little item that I had foolishly not considered, despite all my planning.

My eyes filled with tears at the frustration of it all. Will had been right, I thought, angrily wiping away the tears: my harebrained scheme indeed.

As I slid into my seat a few minutes later, just in time for second lesson, James glanced over at me.

"You said you'd be well again by second lesson, and now I see that you are," he said. "I guess you were right. You do know your own body."

It was all I could do not to laugh out loud.

I survived several days of my own inconvenient bleeding, but I was still miffed at James for saying Will's letter was a pack of lies. Just because he appeared to have forgiven me for my exasperating behavior, returning to his usual state of unflappable calm, did not mean I had to be equally forgiving. Now that I was reassured that we were still some form of friends, I'd taken to spending more time with Little.

Sundays were always peculiar days at the Betterman Academy, everything feeling slightly off from the strict routine of the other six days. Those who didn't have to hurry out of bed early to dress before their roommates saw them had the luxury of lying in bed late. Then there was often an informal cricket match on the playing fields, or perhaps a round of boxing, or even a walk into town for kidney pie and muffins or sausages and scones before the prayer bell rang for chapel at eleven. After chapel, where the headmaster, Dr. Hunter, did have a tendency to go on, there was more free time at our disposal. It was on one such Sunday that I accepted an offer from Little to go fishing.

There was a small river that ran beyond the wooded area on the far side of the playing fields, and supposedly the fishing there was good. Fishing was not something I'd ever done before, but I knew that a lot of the other boys did and I figured it was safe enough for my first time out to go with Little. I'd noticed that Little could be somewhat oblivious to what went on around him, so occupied was he all the time with simply keeping himself as safe as he could from Hamish and Mercy. Little would never notice that I had no clue as to what to do with my fishing gear, that for once someone was watching him in order to learn something.

Though I didn't want to be uncharitable, as we sat on the bank side by side, waiting for something to happen, I could see where Little did present something of a problem. He was certainly kind, compared with most of the other boys, but there was also a vacancy to him. Old Man Peters hadn't much patience with Little's inability to grasp whatever subject was under discussion, and Little earned frequent raps on the knuckles or even a cane over the head. And while I could not condone Old Man Peters's chosen method of showing his displeasure, I could understand his exasperation.

With the possible exception of James, the students at the Betterman Academy were divided into two categories: despots—or bullies—and slaves, the latter category made up of the nervous and the sensitive, the small and the feminine.

I could not bring myself to pursue what was obviously the most lofty goal in the school: to be feared by everybody, as Hamish clearly was, though again with the possible exception of James. But while Little seemed resigned to his lot in the category of the nervous and the sensitive, the small and the feminine, I was determined not to be perceived as any of those things.

"Do you have anything else we might try as bait?" Little asked me.

"Such as what?" I asked. We'd been using worms we'd found on the banks.

"I don't know. I thought maybe you'd thought to bring some bread along or something."

I set aside my fishing gear and rose, turning my trouser pockets inside out. The key to my wardrobe fell to the ground. With a blush and a hasty move, I scooped it up and put it away without a word.

"Sorry," I said, resuming my seat. "'Fraid I didn't think of that. You?"

He shook his head, dejected by the hopelessness of it all. "No."

After a long moment, he said, "Did you know that there was a headmaster here before Dr. Hunter?"

"I assumed as much," I said, "the school being so old."

"And did you know that the previous headmaster is buried under the altar in the chapel?"

"I don't believe I had heard about that."

"It's true." He nodded vehemently, as though I'd told him it was false. "The old headmaster had no family and loved this place so much, he was buried there when he died." He shuddered. "How gruesome!"

I said that there might be worse places to be buried than somewhere one had loved.

"And do you know what's even more horrible?" Little asked as though I'd said nothing.

"No, what?"

"When no one else is around, Hamish makes me go stand near the altar. He says he's sure the old headmaster's head is right under where I'm standing." Little shuddered again. "It gives me nightmares."

Poor Little. Sometimes it was impossible to know just what to say to allay his multitude of fears—not that he didn't have good reason for many of those fears, given how often Hamish tormented him, boxed his ears or cuffed him, kicked him or twisted his arms for the mere sport of it.

Still, Little was mostly inoffensive, and in the absence of any other company, he suited me just fine. At least I knew he was never going to try to put me in a blanket and toss me.

And so we passed a pleasantly lazy Sunday afternoon; pleasant, at least, until late in the day. No fish had taken our bait, and I was just thinking it might be time to start heading back when I heard a threatening sound of rustling leaves coming from deep in the woods behind us.

It was Mercy's voice I heard first.

"I'm sure this is where Stephens said he always goes." His speech sounded slightly slurred. I knew from experience that many of the boys took advantage of the long Sundays to indulge in beer or gin punch.

Stephens often tried to get in good with Hamish and Mercy by telling them things about the other boys.

Hamish's speech sounded equally slurred as he mockingly replied, "How can this be where Stephens says he *always* goes? We're still in the bloody woods, aren't we? I don't see how even *Little* can be fishing in the bloody woods."

"Oh no," Little whispered, true anguish in his face. "They'll throw me in the river when they find me."

"Then we must run away," I said back, not worrying about being overheard by Hamish and Mercy—they were tramping around so loudly and talking at such volume, they couldn't possibly hear anything but themselves.

"There's no point," Little said. "We can never outrun them. Have you ever seen them at cricket? And besides, it's only worse in the end if you try to run."

How awful it must be, I thought, to know such constant fear. I examined my own feelings. Was I happy that at any moment Little and I might be confronted by Hamish and Mercy, with no other students or masters around to temper their behavior? I couldn't say I looked forward to the conflict, but I was not going to literally quake in fear, as Little was now doing.

I remembered thinking earlier that I never wanted to be perceived as nervous and sensitive, small and feminine, and I decided that if swagger was what it took to survive here, even mental swagger, then I would swagger with the best of them.

"Hamish! Mercy!" I shouted in a taunting voice. "Over here!"

"What are you doing?" Little squealed, looking at me as though I'd gone mad.

"You said there was no use, that they'd only catch us sooner or later." I shrugged. "Why not make it sooner, then, and get it over with?"

As the thrashing footsteps came nearer, I grabbed Little's hand and pulled him toward a young tree near the river.

"Come on." I hurried him along, then pointed at the tree and instructed: "Climb."

"But I can't—"

"Climb!"

So used to obeying the commands of others, Little grabbed the lower limbs of the tree and scurried up. As Hamish and Mercy broke through the clearing behind us, I hurried after him, doing my best to avoid the dangers presented by Little's wildly scrambling feet.

We climbed as high as we could, until the tree became too precariously thin near the top.

"Well, that's not very sporting of them." I looked down to see Mercy staring up at us dumbly. "How are we supposed to chase them up a tree?" Mercy looked at Hamish. "We can't run up a tree, can we?"

"Get down from there!" Hamish commanded.

"No," I said simply.

"No?" Hamish hiccupped. "Then I suppose we'll just have to come up."

Hamish grabbed the base of the tree.

"I wouldn't try that if I were you," I advised.

"You wouldn't—"

"No. You're too big. By the time you reach where we are, the weight of you will snap the top off. And while it's true that that might cause *us* to fall to our deaths, it's entirely possible that the dead one could turn out to be *you.*"

Despite my warning, Hamish did come a ways up, the tree bending back and forth wildly all the while. I don't know what stopped him, if it was that furious shaking—which couldn't have been much fun in his pixilated state, I was certain, having been pixilated myself once before—or if it finally sank in that he could get himself hurt. Whatever the case, he let go of the tree and dropped to earth with a thud.

"We could try to shake them out," Mercy suggested.

Which they tried to do for several long minutes, and which was no fun for Little and me as we hung on for dear life.

But when it became apparent we would not be dislodged, they got tired of that occupation.

I wondered what means they might try next.

Near the river were several stones, some small, some quite large. It occurred to me to worry that—

"Here!" Mercy cried to Hamish, catching sight of the same potential weapons I'd been looking at.

Mercy and Hamish both seized stones and took aim. Soon I felt the tree sway in concert with Little's own fearful shaking, causing me to hold on tighter—honestly, in that moment it felt as though Little presented the greater danger! But he needn't have been so scared. The two boys below us were so drunk, their shots went wide of the mark, which only made them that much more determined, that much more angry.

With each missed shot, the stones grew bigger, the anger more obvious. Then Mercy did get off a throw that might have done real damage, only it struck against a knot in the tree, ricocheted off, and went straight at Mercy's forehead.

"Ouch!" Mercy cried, one hand going instinctively to his wound while he shook the fist of the other hand at me, as though it had all been my fault. Then he turned to Hamish. "Maybe this isn't such a good idea after all?"

"Well, we did tree them," Hamish proclaimed manfully.

"We should just wait here," Mercy said, still rubbing his forehead. "Eventually, they'll have to come down."

"Don't count on it," I said cheerily.

Ignoring me, they settled on the ground beneath the tree, seemingly content to wait us out.

So that was how an hour or more passed, the four of us locked in a stalemate as the day disappeared.

Then the first warning bell for calling-over came.

Calling-over was the ritual that ended each day proper at the Betterman Academy. Prior to dinner, we were all required to appear in the chapel, where the masters would walk up and down the middle aisle yelling, "Silence! Silence!" Then each boy was called by name and was expected to respond "Here!" Missing calling-over was a grave offense, and there was only a quarter of an hour to assume one's position between the first calling-over bell and the last.

"You'd better go," I taunted Hamish and Mercy. "You don't want to be late."

"The rules apply to you too," Mercy pointed out.

"Rules are made by the masters as challenges," I said blithely. "It would be bad form not to try to break them. It's almost what they want us to do."

"Yes," Hamish said, "but getting caught breaking the rules leads to punishment. So now you have no choice but to come down."

"Of course we have a choice," I countered calmly. "And today, Christopher and I choose to be late."

"Christopher?" Hamish was confused.

"Little," I said. "His name's Christopher."

There was a hurried consultation as Hamish and Mercy debated what to do: wait for us to get down—eventually, we would have to go to the privy, they decided—in which case we'd all get in trouble, or run for it.

"You probably only have ten minutes now," I said. "Are you sure you can run that fast in your condition?"

Hamish gave the tree one last great shake.

"Thanks for stopping by!" I yelled after them as they took off through the woods.

Little looked at me then as though I was either the craziest person he'd ever met or his own personal hero, perhaps both.

"You do realize, don't you," he said, "that we're going to get in very big trouble for this and that Hamish will hate you forever?"

"Yes, well," I replied, with a bluff confidence I was no longer certain I felt, "but wasn't it worth it?"

CHAPTER *seven*

October 1, 18—

Dear Will,

It has come to my attention that the letter you wrote me was peppered with lies. I suppose I could return the favor—or the insult—by telling you lies as well, telling you that everything is wonderful here, that the food is the finest of cuisines and the boys the most capital of fellows. But you, having been at school if not at this particular school, would see right through that, would you not? And so, I will instead say . . .

You might have warned me what school was really like! Yes, you did tell me about the food; I will grant you that. But you might have told me how the boys are more interested in terrorizing one another than in pursuing anything lofty, like, say, the reason we are all supposed to be here—you know, education? You might have said how hard it is to keep one's eyes on that goal when all around, one is distracted by the constant inanity of boys tossing each other in blankets, persecuting one another for poor singing, getting treed by the river—yes, all three have already happened to me—and otherwise jockeying for superior position.

The truth of the matter is, I *do* love the learning aspect of being here. I love Shakespeare even more than I did when I read to your great-uncle—in particular I love all the plays that deal with women masquerading as men, for obvious reasons—and I have grown to love Dickens, with all his coincidences; how something you think does not matter in chapter 1 turns out to be quite critical before the author rings down the curtain with his "finis." I love the Greek and Latin, although it took me quite some time to master the different characters of the former. I even love the vulgus! But no sooner do I immerse myself in one of those things I have developed such a passion for than some new idiocy presents itself to draw me away. Who would have guessed that one of the chief barriers to getting a good education is being at an actual school? Still, I suppose the opportunity is the key. And I would never have thought of the need to master Greek so that I could read works in the original if I had never come here.

My roommate, an annoyingly self-sufficient—dare I say self-absorbed?—boy named James Tyler, is also a great distraction.

Despite the lies in your letter, I do hope that wherever you are, you are being treated well and that you are happy.

Oh, before I close, I have one last bone to pick with you: I SHOULD THINK YOU MIGHT HAVE WARNED ME ABOUT COMPULSORY SPORTS!!!

Your sister in spirit, despite all your lies about where you are and pertinent omissions about school,
Bet

It was full dark by the time Little and I made our way back to Proctor Hall that night, dragging our fishing gear behind us. At Little's insistence, we'd waited in the tree a long time after Hamish and Mercy had left us, to ensure that they did not lie in wait; it was Little's great fear that they might change their minds and decide that getting punished for the crime of missing calling-over was a price worth paying if it meant the opportunity to torment us some more. I personally thought Little insane for thinking this. As far as I could tell, Hamish and Mercy were too drunk for such a complex weighing of options, never mind that I suspected that both were sound and fury, signifying nothing, and would never risk their own necks if it could be avoided. But Little refused to accept my reasoning. Little, in his fear, refused to leave the tree.

And I refused to leave Little.

So it was that, by the time we made it back to Proctor Hall, final calling-over had long since passed, and the others were no doubt nearly done with supper. Mr. Winter, having had to stay behind to wait for us, thus missing his own supper, did not look happy.

"Dr. Hunter says that you are to go up to the house and wait for him," Mr. Winter informed us. "As soon as supper is over, he will deal with you directly."

We were at the door when Mr. Winter's next words stopped us. "I do hope your backsides can withstand the beating."

I had never been in a headmaster's house before. I had never even exchanged words with Dr. Hunter though I had been at school for over a month.

The headmaster's residence, even with its round tower and its flag flying proudly above it, was not at all impressive when taken in comparison with Grangefield Hall, but it was certainly far grander than Proctor Hall. I suppose a combination of formal and cozy would be the best way to describe it. The lines of the furniture in the room we were led to were severe, as though to discourage visitors from staying long, and yet on those same pieces of furniture one occasionally glimpsed a needlepoint pillow bearing some sort of cheery legend. The combination of severe lines and comfortable cushions delivered a contradictory message. I suspected the needlepoint was the handiwork of Mrs. Hunter, a handsome woman of about thirty years of age whom I'd only ever seen during chapel; Mrs. Hunter was apparently wise enough to avoid the chaos that characterized every dining experience in Marchand Hall.

As we waited for Dr. Hunter to arrive, Little quaked in fear and I tried to get Little to stop quaking in fear.

"I don't think they've ever actually *killed* anyone here for being late to supper," I joked.

For some reason, that failed to help.

Seeing the headmaster as he entered, his open black robe flowing behind him, his don's cap firmly on his head, I thought that Dr. Hunter had much in common with the appointments of that room.

He was about a decade older than his wife, had black hair graying at the temples, and was easily the tallest man I'd ever met. He was also extraordinarily lean, that leanness giving him an air of severity that was consonant with the furniture about us, and his jaw looked as strong as a mallet. But his eyes . . . They were very dark, almost black, yet a light danced in them, and as he greeted us with two brisk nods—"Warren; Gardener"—I could have sworn I saw a smile tugging at the edges of that mouth, the teeth beyond those lips strong and white.

"What is the meaning of this?" he demanded, all traces of any smile disappearing. "You do realize, do you not, that missing calling-over is a grave offense? What possible excuse can you have?"

"MacPherson and Mercy, sir," I started, but then a shocking thing happened. Little, who rarely spoke to anyone unless he absolutely had to, cut me off.

"We were out f-f-fishing, sir," he said boldly; or, at least, that halting delivery of some sort of speech was bold for Little. "The fish weren't biting. We wanted to catch a fish, and so we stayed out too late. The fault is entirely our own, and we gladly accept any p-p-punishment you deem fit."

I snapped my head toward my companion. What was Little *doing?* I wondered. Yes, technically, we had knowingly stayed out late, but it wasn't our fault. There had been very good reasons.

"Of course you do," Dr. Hunter barked back, but when I turned to look at him, his eyes weren't on Little. They were on me.

"I do understand that when boys go fishing, they like to catch something," Dr. Hunter went on. "Be that as it may, flouting the rules in favor of the possibility of catching trout cannot be tolerated."

I could almost feel Little commence to trembling even more beside me. No doubt he was terrified at the prospect of the beating Mr. Winter had warned us about.

"You will each memorize forty lines of Homer a day for the next two weeks; I will be by to test you on them nightly. What's more, you will be confined to your rooms for that same period except for essential activities. Essential activities means lessons, eating, and sports. Essential activities does *not* mean singing with your friends in the great room on Saturday nights. It does not mean going into town on the weekends. And it certainly does not mean going fishing." Dr. Hunter paused. "If there is a second offense—and I trust there will not be—the punishment will be more severe."

Poor Little. He couldn't help himself. "You mean you're not going to beat us?" he asked.

Dr. Hunter looked like thunder as he lowered his face down to Little's level and barked, *"Go!"*

Little scampered off, obviously relieved that things hadn't gone any worse, but I remained behind.

"Was there something you wished to speak with me about?" The headmaster looked at me, some small amusement in his eyes. "Were you perhaps expecting a beating too?"

As the headmaster had been detailing our punishment, I'd had a chance to think on why Little had cut me off, why he wouldn't allow me to inform Dr. Hunter of Hamish and Mercy's involvement in our misadventure. Clearly, he feared reprisals. And perhaps they would have wanted revenge. But I was sure I had seen that glimpse of a smile on Dr. Hunter's face when he first walked in. Surely if he knew the true state of affairs here at the Betterman Academy, if he was made aware of how relentlessly Little was persecuted by the others, he would take decisive action to put an end to it.

"No, sir," I said at last. "But I did want to say that while, yes, it was our own fault that we were late this evening, it was not entirely our own fault. MacPherson and Mercy—"

"Yes, you started to say something about them earlier, but then Little cut you off."

"He cut me off, sir, because he is terrified of them! He fears that if you were told the truth about what happened this evening, MacPherson and Mercy would exact their revenge."

"The truth? And what truth might that be?"

"They deliberately followed him down to the river for the sole purpose of committing mischief. We had to climb a tree just to escape them! And it was obvious that if we had come down while they were still there, at best we would have been thrown in the river; at worst, grave bodily damage would have ensued. That is the thing, sir! They are bullies, and they are forever persecuting Little, more than anyone else. He lives in a constant state of fear from them, going to bed at night and rising still trembling. I worry that if something is not done—"

"Are you aware, Gardener, that *I* am aware of your record at the previous schools you have attended?"

I had been so caught up in the passion of my narrative I had missed the fact that what slight amusement there had been in Dr. Hunter's eyes at the beginning of our tête-à-tête had dissipated. I saw now that it was no longer there.

"I suppose, if I had thought about it . . ." I couldn't help it. I did squirm a bit.

"So I am aware of the lying and the cheating and the general mischief—the fights and all that—although I must confess, I have yet to suss out why it was you left your last school. Be that as it may, nothing in your record caused me to believe the worst of you—boys, after all, will be boys—but this? I never suspected that you would be that worst sort of boy: a teller of tales against your mates."

"Sir?"

"The best thing a boy can hope for from any school is to be marked down as having good character. Well, your actions tonight shall result in a *loss* of character. Your punishment is hereby increased to sixty lines of Homer, and I hope never to have such a discussion with you again. You should know, Gardener, that schools have run quite nicely for centuries on the system currently in place, and they have done so without your help." He nodded once, curtly. "Consider yourself dismissed."

I turned away with a heavy heart, filled with dejection. Whatever might ultimately save Little from the constant state of misery he lived in, it would not come from this quarter.

I confess that, as it turned out, I did not mind my punishment. When Dr. Hunter came by to test me on my memorized lines, I was always ready for him, and every now and then I could see approval in the way he looked at me. No more was said about what I'd tried to discuss with him that night at his residence. And although most of the other boys would have resented two weeks of being confined to their rooms for anything other than essential activities, I didn't mind that either. In fact, I found it a relief not to have to go to the great room on Saturday night and sing poorly and then be tossed in a blanket for my efforts, nor did I mind not being able to go for a stroll after supper or into town on Sunday. I enjoyed the time alone, time to spend on studying and, since it was now easy to finish my lessons early, as there were no other distractions, time to spend reading for the sheer pleasure of it. And of course, I wasn't really alone, for nearly every moment I was in the room, James was there as well. As I worked silently, he worked silently. As I read silently, he read silently. And so it went.

It wasn't until the second Sunday of my punishment, after I heard him refuse an offer to go into town with some of the others for the second week in a row, that it occurred to me that James might be staying in on my account.

Did he feel that sorry for me? I wondered. Did he worry that if left on my own for too long, I might do something dire to myself? Whatever the case, I now felt responsible for his self-imposed lack of freedom. And so, for the first time since my confinement began, I sought to engage him in conversation.

It helped that there was something on my mind.

"Why is everyone here?" I wondered aloud.

I was sitting at my desk and had turned in my seat to ask the question. James was lying on his side on his bed, head propped up on one elbow as he read Alexandre Dumas's *The Three Musketeers.*

He looked up now. "That's a rather existential question for a Sunday," he observed.

"I didn't mean it like that," I said, feeling a blush color my cheeks. "I meant that the Betterman Academy is so"—and here I recalled Paul Gardener's words for it—"*last ditch.* No one appears to be greatly interested in the learning aspect of the place, except for me. And possibly you," I added grudgingly.

"Thank you," he said, just as grudgingly.

"But what of those others? What did they do to land themselves here?"

James yawned, even though it was still only early afternoon. "The usual reasons, for the most part. Hamish and Mercy, as you well know, are villains. They no doubt got sent down from their previous schools for similar reasons as the ones that brought, well, *you* here: lying, cheating, general mischief. Although I do suspect there was more violence on their parts."

"And Little?"

"Surely you've noticed that Little is, um, a little dull?"

I nodded.

"That's it, then. I know it's not nice to say, but it is the truth: Little was too slow for the other schools he went to."

"And how about you?" I said. "What are you doing here?"

He yawned again. "What are any of us doing here, really?"

There was something odd about that yawn—forced, almost too casual—and his choice of words. It was obvious to me that he was trying to deflect the question. But why? Why wouldn't he want me to know why he was here? Then it occurred to me: I would never want him to know the real truth of why *I* was here! What if my questions started him asking questions? I certainly couldn't have *that.* And so I did the expected schoolboy thing, countered indifferent sarcasm with indifferent sarcasm. "Now who's being existential?" I asked.

But he ignored me. He swung his legs around and pulled himself up so he was sitting on the edge of his bed. "Since you've decided to be in a talkative mood today, let *me* ask *you* something."

"Yes?" I suddenly felt cautious.

"What happened during your meeting with Hunter that night you came in late?"

"Oh, that!" I laughed. It was a relief that he wasn't going to quiz me on any of my peculiar habits—how I dressed and undressed in total darkness, how sometimes the supply of washcloths mysteriously diminished—and it was a relief finally to talk about it with someone.

So I told him the whole story, everything from when Little and I first heard Hamish and Mercy tramping through the woods to the point where Dr. Hunter dismissed me.

"You *idiot!*" he said when I'd completed my tale. "How could you do something so *stupid?*" Despite his having nothing physical in common with Will except gender, James looked and sounded shockingly like him when he said that.

"Excuse me?"

"You're supposed to be so . . . *worldly,* Will! Aren't you the boy that's been sent down for more crimes than anyone here?"

I nodded in acknowledgment of my assumed résumé.

"Then how could you not know such a simple thing?" he went on. "How could you possibly think that you would tell Hunter and then, oh, I don't know—what? abracadabra?—he'd make it all go away?"

When he put it like that . . .

"Yes," I said, feeling the need to defend my actions, "but have you ever seen all those bruises Little gets? Or how he lives in terror? And he's right to feel that way! If someone doesn't do something about it, one day Hamish and Mercy might accidentally *kill* him!"

"And you think that the way to stop this is to tell one of the masters or Hunter? How can someone with your experiences possibly be so naive?"

For obvious reasons, I chose not to answer that.

"I don't care what you say," I said. "Something has to be done."

"I'll tell you one thing."

"And that is?" I clenched my fists at my sides. I was prepared to fight longer, all day if I had to.

"You may be stupid, but I admire your spirit."

Now I really didn't know what to say.

James stretched out on his bed again, resumed the position he'd been in before, and picked up his book.

"Would you like to read this when I'm done with it?" he offered. "It's awfully good."

"That would be nice," I said, unsure how to take what he'd apparently meant as a compliment: I was a stupid person with spirit.

"Oh," he said, idly turning a page, "I've never asked you: what compulsory sport do you intend to pursue here?"

Oof!

It was amazing how the air got knocked out of one when one's chest hit the ground hard, one's body having been thrown to the cold earth by some unseen opponent.

I should have known that cricket would not be the sport for me.

True, I'd looked downright natty when I'd put on my uniform a few hours previous: the crisp white trousers; the jaunty cap and jersey that were a colorful red and royal purple, the house colors of Proctor Hall; the untanned yellow cricket shoes on my feet. But for once I should have heeded Little's endless fears.

"Cricket is a violent sport," he'd squeaked at me. "There are injuries all the time. Bruises, broken collarbones, even lamings!"

I'd scoffed at the idea of the lamings, but as I spat dirt out of my mouth now, I was scoffing no longer.

The uses of the ball, the bat, the wickets—like Casca said in *Julius Caesar* about Cicero's speech, it was all Greek to me.

So I spent the day mostly trying to avoid the sports implements entirely, running around on the field as far away as I could get from the main action, the mess of boys chasing and pushing and kicking after a leather ball as incomprehensible to me as the military maneuvers and fighting of Will's beloved wars.

"Look at Gardener," I heard Hamish say to Mercy at one point. "He's even worse than Little. Why, he runs like *a girl!*"

I resented that remark, even as I resembled it.

"We should tackle him," Mercy suggested.

"But he's on our team!" Stephens objected.

Whatever Mercy said in reply, I didn't hear. Ignoring the constant refrain of Little that was ringing in my head—"If you run, you only make it worse on yourself in the end"—I ran. Mercy must have responded with something persuasive, though, for before I knew it, I was hurled to the ground again, the weight of Hamish full on my back.

I felt his hot breath close to my ear as he spoke: "This isn't really your game, is it?"

One thing I knew for certain, I was *not* going to remove my jacket and waistcoat, roll up my sleeves, arrange for a second, and put on gloves in order to try boxing.

Fencing!

Cricket required playing on a side, being part of a team, something I clearly wasn't cut out for. But fencing? *That* you played for yourself.

I'd read all about fencing in *The Three Musketeers,* James having loaned it to me as promised when he was finished with it. How hard could it be? True, in Dumas's story, the characters were always running the risk of death. But that was because they were fencing in their regular clothes. The very *idea* was to do damage to your opponent! But no one was going to be fighting a real *duel* here—we were simply boys playing compulsory sports at school! Surely they would provide us with protective clothing so that no one would get seriously hurt?

For once, I was right about something.

There *was* protective clothing. There was a white uniform—once again, I looked natty—underneath which was a variety of thick gear to offer protection to different body parts. There was even a mask with a mesh front to protect the face, and a bib extending down from the mask so that no neck skin was vulnerable. There were gloves to keep the foils from dangerously finding their ways up tempting sleeves. Really, there were no openings anywhere that the foil could pierce. And if there were? The tips of the foils—which were disturbingly sharp; I checked—were covered by little balls so they could do no damage.

This was sport of the best kind, a gentleman's sport, I thought to myself as I faced off against Hamish. Hamish, unlike the other boys, who practiced only one sport, engaged in every sport he could make time for in addition to cricket. I had one hand on my hip, foil raised, our mates from Proctor Hall gathered around us.

"En garde!" I shouted, fancying myself D'Artagnan as I brandished my weapon at my enemy. I was determined to thrust and parry my

way to victory. I didn't need to be a good runner for this sport. I didn't need to know any silly rules about balls and bats and wickets. All I needed was to be more agile than my opponent, which I was, I soon saw. Fencing, I quickly realized, didn't involve any regular sort of speed. Rather, it involved the vision to see where your opponent was going so that you could parry his attack or gracefully move out of the way of his thrust, preferably while making a connecting thrust of your own.

I could do this!

I could *beat* Hamish at this!

What I hadn't counted on was Hamish's anger.

What I hadn't counted on was that Hamish could occasionally be in control of that anger, waiting until the fencing master was distracted by a diversion caused by Mercy and Stephens that gave Hamish just enough time to turn his weapon in reverse and move in close to pummel my body with the hilt of his weapon.

It was the blow to my head that knocked me out, briefly.

I came to only to find James and Little carrying me across the commons, in the direction of Proctor Hall.

"I'm fine," I insisted.

I was lying, of course. I was doing the expected schoolboy thing: pretending events didn't matter, when they did; behaving as if being beaten viciously was of little import, something to be met with an unflappable exterior.

But on the inside?

On the inside I was badly shaken, scared, terrified even, just thinking of what had happened.

At the pub with Will that night, that night that seemed so long ago now, he had warned me that school might be a dangerous place for me. But had I listened? No. The worst I could imagine back then was being exposed as a girl and finding myself sent down as a result. It had never occurred to me, not in my wildest nightmares, that as a boy I might find myself physically beaten so ruthlessly.

Yes, I had been tossed in a blanket. Yes, Little and I had been treed by the river. Both had been unpleasant affairs, even unsettling, but neither had been anything like this.

No one had laid a hand on me in anger in my entire life.

I wanted to run, run away—well, if I *could* run, which I could not, given how badly bruised my whole body was. Still, I wanted to get away from the Betterman Academy as quickly as I could, put this, all of it, behind me. I had been silly to think I could impersonate a boy, foolish to believe that my dream of an education could ever be a reality. I would—

And then anger came in.

What was I going to do, become like *Little?* Live in fear of the likes of *Hamish?* Oh, no. I had worked too hard, come too far—they would *not* take this away from me.

"I'm fine," I insisted again as James and Little carried me up the stairs of Proctor Hall to the door of Mrs. Smithers's rooms.

When she asked them what had happened, they told her that a contest had simply gotten a little too zealous.

Despite the pain I was in—did Hamish have to hit me so many times? and so hard?—I could see that she didn't believe them. But what could she do? It would be the same back at the scene we'd just left. The boys would tell the fencing master that it was an accident that I'd been injured so badly, perhaps even blame my lack of skills for what had befallen me, and the fencing master would have no choice but to take them at their word. In fact, he'd no doubt be relieved to have avoided a moral dilemma, for what would he have been compelled to do if brought face to face with the knowledge that one boy had intentionally caused grievous bodily harm to another? We all knew the lay of the land at the Betterman Academy. The very worst crime one could commit was to tell on someone else.

Even I knew that now.

"Leave us," Mrs. Smithers commanded James and Little, looking more annoyed than I'd ever seen her. I wondered if she was frustrated that she'd been lied to about what had happened. Perhaps she held James and Little partly responsible for their complicity in those lies?

Whatever the case, they took their leave after James had put his hand on my shoulder and assured me I would be all right, and Mrs. Smithers closed the door behind them and turned the key in the lock.

"I'm fine," I insisted yet again as she removed my fencing mask.

"Take everything off," she said, ignoring my words.

"What?" I said, unsure if I had understood her. She couldn't mean . . .

"Your clothes," she said harshly. "How can I possibly treat your injuries, how can I even tell how severe those injuries are, if you keep your clothes on?" She put her hands on her wide hips. "There's no need for modesty. I can assure you, Gardener, that in my time at the Betterman Academy, I've seen many a boy naked."

CHAPTER *eight*

I remained seated, frozen to the spot.

"Well, Gardener," Mrs. Smithers said when I refused to move, "are you going to take off your clothes or am I going to have to take them off for you?"

At last, as though a mesmerist were controlling my actions, I slowly began undoing my fencing tunic, one excruciating button at a time. Then the protective gear, moving slightly quicker now. By the time I got to the last layer of covering between my body and the world, the material that bound my breasts tight, my fingers were working with rapid speed to remove the mummy casing. It was as though it had finally struck me that the end was near, my exposure imminent, and now I simply wanted to be done with it.

In truth, after the battering I'd received at Hamish's hands, it felt good to be free like that. And hadn't I not so very long ago been contemplating leaving anyway?

I sat in my chair, trousers still on, my mummy material dangling uselessly from my fingers, and waited for doom to fall on me. And yet, curiously, I felt a strange combination of defiance and detached acceptance about it all. If I'd ever given the matter enough thought, surely I would have realized that eventually it would come to this. Or if not exactly this, then some form of it. *Let whatever is to happen, happen,* I thought.

Mrs. Smithers barely glanced at my upper body, perhaps both shocked and embarrassed at the sight of my semi-nakedness, before turning away from me to fill a basin with water. Then she took a cloth, immersed it in the water, and began gently bathing my injuries.

Hamish's efforts had not broken the skin anywhere, I saw now, but there were more bruises than I could count, the coloration of those bruises already changing to a startling array of hues, angry purples and reds and sickening yellows.

As the cloth made contact with my skin, I involuntarily flinched back, from both the coldness of the cloth and the sensation of pressure against my injuries.

"Sorry," Mrs. Smithers apologized curtly. "If I'd known one of you boys was going to get yourself half killed today, I'd have made sure to heat some water in preparedness. As it is . . ."

"One of you *boys*"? Was Mrs. Smithers insane? Was she blind? Could she not see that, whatever else I might be, I was not "one of you boys"?

"Whoever did this," Mrs. Smithers went on when I did not speak, beginning to apply some sort of ointment to the tender skin covering my ribs, "wanted to do as much damage as possible."

Of course she was right, there had been grave malice in Hamish's behavior, but what was going on here? Why was Mrs. Smithers not acting shocked? Why was she not sounding the alarm, sending for the housemaster, sending for the *head*master? Why was she not . . .

No, I told myself. Of course she wouldn't do that, *couldn't* do that while I was still half naked. It wouldn't be proper. She would wait until after she'd finished ministering to me, and *then* she would turn me in. It was only a matter of minutes now, I thought, as she began to wrap cloth around my ribs, cloth not dissimilar to that which dangled from my fingers.

"It'll hurt even more in the morning than it does now," she cautioned as she worked, "but if you keep this dressing on it, you should heal nicely in no time." She paused, gave the matter some thought. "No, you won't heal in no time, but you will eventually heal. There."

As Mrs. Smithers had worked, her fingers had moved with deftness, and yet I'd also felt a roughness to her gestures, as though she were angry at something. I'd assumed she was angry with me for my idiocy and my lies. But now, as she reached down and gently pried the dangling fabric from my fingers, I felt a change. Perhaps she pitied me for the mortification that was about to come?

"Here," she said softly. "You'll be wanting this again."

"What?" I said dumbly.

Why was she . . . ? But then I thought, *Of course. She's giving me my things back because she can't very well parade me through the school naked.*

I began to wrap the fabric around myself, wincing with the effort; Hamish had assaulted my back as well.

"Perhaps I can help you with that," Mrs. Smithers offered.

Without waiting for an answer, she took the fabric and gently began winding it around my upper body, careful to avoid any contact that might be indelicate. Then she helped me back into the fencing tunic.

"I don't think you need the protective gear anymore," she said as she did up the buttons, "but you'll be wanting to keep yourself covered with this, at least until you get back to your room." She finished the last button. I had the peculiar sensation that I was being dressed like a doll. "There," she said a second time, clearly pleased with herself.

"What is going on here?" I burst out, the first words I'd spoken, other than the dumb "What," since she'd told me to take off my clothes.

"I'm sorry?" She looked puzzled.

"You're sending me back to *my room* now? But I don't understand. Are you going to send for Dr. Hunter and have him go there? Or are you just going to call a carriage to take me away?"

"Why would I do either of those things?" Mrs. Smithers looked more puzzled still.

God! Did I have to say everything myself? "Because I'm *a girl!*" I half shouted at her in my exasperation.

"Oh." She paused. "That."

"Yes!" For some strange reason, I felt like throttling her. "That!"

"But why would I turn you in now?"

"Because you've just learned—"

"Is that what you think?" And then she laughed, practically in my face, the first real mirth I'd ever seen Mrs. Smithers show. "You actually think—" She struggled to control herself, but it appeared useless. "You actually thought—"

"I fail to see the humor in the current situation," I said, the sternness of my words useless in the face of her gales of laughter.

Oddly, I think it was my use of the word *humor* that sobered her.

"No," she admitted at last, "the current situation is not funny. It is merely funny that you think I am only just today discovering that you are a girl."

I narrowed my eyes at her. "How long have you known?"

"How long?" She looked at me as though I'd said something particularly dense. "Do you think I'm stupid?"

"Do I think you're—"

"I've known since you brought those sheets to me! Impetigo, my foot. What kind of fool story was that to tell me? What was it you said, that when you were younger you had it so bad you used to bleed like a geyser? Believe me, I know a little bit about medical matters, and I know impetigo doesn't work on a body like *that.*"

"So that's what clued you in?"

"Well, that and the quality of the blood on the sheets. I am a woman, after all, Gardener; I do know that a certain kind of blood looks different than others."

I didn't understand. She'd known all this time, and she hadn't turned me in?

"What is your real name anyway?" she asked when I failed to speak.

"It's Elizabeth." I spoke haltingly. "It's Elizabeth Smith. But some call me Bet."

"Bet." She smiled. "Such a pretty nickname." Then she turned brusque again, becoming all business as she handed me the protective fencing items. "You'd best be off now, Gardener."

I had no idea what to make of all this.

"You mean you're really not going to turn me in?" I wondered out loud.

"Turn you in?" she said. "Are you joking with me?" She laughed again. "I happen to think it's the most marvelous thing I've ever heard of!"

I made my way back to my room, still stunned, hearing Mrs. Smithers's words echoing in my mind.

"In my time at Betterman," she'd said, "I thought I'd seen everything, but I've never seen anything to top this. A girl masquerading as a boy to get an education? My hat's off to you, Bet, and I'll do whatever I can to help—I think it's great to see one of *us* putting one over on one of *them* for a change. But do be more careful, won't you? Perhaps I should tell your masters that compulsory sports are out of the question for you for the time being? At least that should minimize one of your risks of exposure."

James was seated at his desk. He turned when he heard me enter, his expression miserable.

"Are you all right?" he said anxiously, rising. "You were gone so long, I feared you might be even more injured than you seemed." He took a step toward me, then stopped himself, as though fearful that if he touched me, perhaps laid a hand on my shoulder, he would cause me greater damage. I was grateful that he did not touch me, for if he had, I would surely have broken down in tears: tears for the shock of physical pain; tears for the frustration of having been unable to defend myself against Hamish; tears of relief that I hadn't been exposed, had been granted a reprieve. I could not allow myself to cry in front of him; even though I thought tears were a perfectly reasonable response in these circumstances, it was not what a boy would do. Certainly, it was not what the kind of boy I had decided I would be—*had* to be—would do.

"What did Smithers say?" James asked when I failed to respond immediately.

"She says that I am to be excused from compulsory sports for the time being, which is, I suppose, a good thing, given that I apparently have no talents in that area." I tried a brave, manly laugh, but the effort caused me to wince as it sparked a seizing pain in my ribs. "She says I will live."

"I suppose that is a good thing as well," James said, attempting to put his own brave smile on it. "Here, sit." He pulled out my chair for me. Having seen my wince, he was all solicitousness now.

"I'm sorry I did not do more to help earlier," he said once I was seated.

Without him having to expand on that, I knew what he was talking about. He was talking about his—and everyone else's—failure to intervene when Hamish was pummeling me.

"It is all right," I said, absolving him now. "We all know that would only have made matters worse."

"Yes," he said, but he did not look relieved at this acknowledgment.

"Do not fear," I said. "Eventually, I'm not sure how yet, I will have my revenge on Hamish."

"I have no doubt that you will."

I wondered if he believed that, if he believed in me.

"Can I get you anything?" he asked.

"No," I said. "All I want to do right now is get out of this fencing costume, since I am no longer to be a fencer."

"Do you need any help?" he offered.

I thought of what that would be like, having James help me undress. Curiously enough, it was not an unpleasant thought. But no. I had survived being exposed to Mrs. Smithers. I could not be so lucky twice, never mind the impropriety of it all.

"That is all right," I said. "I can manage. Now, if you would just . . ." I indicated the door with a nod of my head.

"Oh, right," he said, smiling for the first time since my return. "My roommate who is too shy to take his clothes off in front of anybody. Still, are you sure you don't need me to—"

"Go, James. Please."

He went.

But, oh, how a part of me wished that he could stay.

October turned into November turned into the early dark days of December.

After the fencing incident, I had become something of a pariah among the other boys. It was as though my physical humiliation had been so great, in no small part because of the spectacularly public nature of it, that the others feared proximity to me might cause them to catch the same disease. Even Hamish and Mercy avoided me in the initial aftermath. It would have been nice to think they did so out of shame at having gone too far and because they did not want to hurt me any further. But somehow, I did not think this was the case. Rather, I believed they feared their own exposure. Hamish had managed to do so much damage to me because Mercy and Stephens had distracted the fencing master. But they might not be so lucky a second time. And it would reflect poorly on them if they were caught physically damaging a boy who had already been so . . . *accidentally* injured.

Although they were careful to avoid me, I was not careful to avoid them. Indeed, I actively sought them out. I did this for two reasons: one, revenge for my own sake; and two, revenge for Little's sake, for they had steadily increased their efforts against him.

And so, whenever we were waiting in line to enter chapel or some such place, I made my way to a position behind Hamish and Mercy and elbowed them hard in the ribs or kicked them in the backs of the knees. Then I dropped back into the crowd before they could see me.

Through it all, James remained by my side. He never explained his newfound allegiance to me, but I suspected it stemmed from his guilt about not coming to my aid more forcefully during the fencing incident. So after I dropped back into the crowd following my meager assaults, he assumed my position in line, meaning his was the face Hamish and Mercy saw when they whirled around. It left them frustrated at not being able to fight back; for some reason, they were still intimidated by James. And James was with me one Saturday night when I got it into my head to replace the beer in Mercy's bottles with vinegar that I'd borrowed from Mrs. Smithers.

"The looks on their faces!" Back in our room later on that night, we laughed at the outrage that followed hard on their usual manly swigs.

And James was with me the following night when we scrawled Mercy's and Hamish's names on the outside walls of Proctor Hall, coupled with the most vile of epithets.

And James was most definitely there with me the night before Christmas holiday when we stole into their room in the dead of night, doused the slumbering Hamish and Mercy with buckets of water, and shouted, "For Little!" before racing back to the safety of our own room and breathlessly locking the door behind us.

We collapsed onto our individual beds, laughing, as we listened to the drenched scoundrels' muted curses as they twisted the doorknob. Those curses were no doubt muted because they did not want to rouse Mr. Winter, whose rooms were closer to ours than to theirs and who would not be pleased if awakened, no matter what crime had been committed against them.

"I never would have guessed that first day when I met you," James said, "but I shall miss you over the Christmas holiday."

There was genuine puzzlement in his voice, and I wondered at this. Lately, I'd noticed a warmth in James toward me, and it did not seem to be just because of our newfound camaraderie as partners in crime. It almost seemed—dare I say it?—that he had a sort of attraction toward me, in his looks and in his deeds. But no sooner would I catch a glimpse of such a thing than he would withdraw, as though confused by his own behavior, his own feelings.

I, of course, was not at all confused to find my feelings toward him growing. Daily, he seemed more and more attractive, and not simply because he was so handsome.

But I could say none of that.

"Yes," I finally said, "I suppose I shall miss you too."

Grangefield Hall looked much smaller than the last time I'd seen it, more than three months earlier. But then I wondered: Had the place somehow shrunk, or had I managed to grow larger?

Of course, at least for that first week of my three-week holiday, I was returning to it as Will Gardener. Perhaps that was what made the difference.

It was not just the building that looked so much smaller to me. The old man, who had loomed so large to me not so very long ago, looked smaller now too. More shrunken than I remembered him being, more infirm as well. I worried for the first time: What if something truly awful happened to the real Will Gardener while he was off on his adventure? True, the letters I regularly received from him indicated that he was happy enough and well enough, as much as someone could be in the military. But it was hard to tell what was truth and what were lies. Surely I could not keep up my charade forever, even though I was determined to keep it up at least through the holiday break. But what if the real Will Gardener was injured or, worse, killed? What if something happened and the old man never saw him again?

"Uncle," I greeted him solemnly, feeling the responsibility to succeed in my impersonation more keenly than I had before. Previously, I'd wanted to carry it off for my own sake, so as not to be caught out. But now I wanted to carry it off for his.

"My boy," he said warmly, holding out a gnarled hand to me.

"It is good to be home," I said.

As I spoke the words, I realized how true they were. It was a relief to be away, at least for the time being, from the problem of Hamish and Mercy. It was a relief to be free of the responsibility of Little. It was even a relief to be free of the attraction I felt toward James, and of his for me. I wondered briefly, wildly: Could James like boys? In a way that was, well, contrary to my liking of him?

I shook off those thoughts as the old man indicated I should take a seat beside him.

"Tell me," he said, "how things have been going for you at school."

That sense of relief once again flooded me: relief that, at least for now, rather than having to fool five hundred boys, I had to fool only one old man.

And a handful of servants.

I arrived so late that first night that I did not see any of the servants, but I did not have to wait long for a problem to arise.

The biggest servant hurdle came the following morning, just as I was waking for the first time in Will's spacious bedroom, in Will's spacious bed.

I opened my eyes to the sight of Wiggins, Will's manservant, puttering around the room. In my long journey home in the carriage, alone this time, I had given great thought to how I would behave around the maids now that I was Will: the need to combine an air of entitlement with a basic casual geniality, even a little harmless flirting. But I had forgotten all about Wiggins, perhaps because he had only ever belonged to Will's world, and not at all to mine.

Wiggins was old; ancient, really. Wiggins was so old, the maids often joked that he had been the old man's manservant when *he* was a child.

"I have drawn your bath, sir," Wiggins said, finally noticing that my eyes were wide open. He came to attention at the side of the bed as though waiting for something.

"That is, er, good," I said, holding the sheets firmly at my neck. "Thank you."

Still, he stood. Honestly, he was so old, it was a wonder he didn't tip over as he swayed there.

"Is there something more?" I asked.

"Of course, sir. I am waiting for you."

"Waiting for me? To do what?"

"Why, to get out of bed and get into the bath." He paused, as though trying to remember what came next. "And then I will help you get dressed."

Well, *that* certainly wouldn't do!

"You know what, Wiggins?" I said, forcing a smile. "When I am at school, I do not have the luxury of a manservant, let alone one as efficient as you. The sad truth is, I am used to doing certain things for myself, and I should like to go on doing so now that, er, I am practically a man."

Wiggins looked scandalized. "But you never felt that way when you returned from school before."

"Well, I do now," I asserted vehemently, feeling very masculine.

Wiggins looked worse than scandalized. He looked confused. "But if I am not helping you dress, what shall I be doing?"

"You will be a man of leisure, Wiggins!" I announced, feeling most beneficent.

"A man of leisure?" Worse than scandalized, worse than confused, he now looked horrified. "You mean I am to be put out on the streets after all these years?"

Oh, dear. Now *I* felt dreadful.

"Of course not, Wiggins," I hurriedly reassured him. "You are too valuable for that. We could never survive without you. But you deserve, I think, a respite from work after all your years of service."

"And what shall I do with this . . . *respite?*"

I tried to think what Will would suggest. "Why, you will flirt with the maids!" I said brightly.

The idea obviously appealed to Wiggins.

"But don't think it'll be like this all the time," I called after him as he hurried to depart. "You never know when I might change my mind and need your services again," I cautioned genially, thinking that if—*when*—Will returned, he would want his manservant back.

Of course, later in the day, when I went down to breakfast and came in contact with the other servants and saw their skeptical looks as they regarded me from behind the master's back, it struck me for the first time: What had Will and I been thinking? Yes, at school, where they were simply expecting *a* Will Gardener but not a *specific* Will Gardener, I'd been able to fool people. And yes, I'd been able to fool poor Wiggins, who was very old and somewhat dotty, and even the master, who was practically blind. But it didn't matter that Will and I shared several physical similarities; I was *shorter* than Will, shaped *different* than Will. How had we ever imagined we could get away with this?

And yet we *did* get away with it. The servants never let on, despite their occasional skeptical glances in my direction, for the old man seemed unaware that anything was out of the ordinary.

Did the servants, I wondered, recognize me beneath my disguise? And more important, *why* didn't they say anything to the old man?

Then I understood: like Will, like me, they simply did not want to cause him any grief.

We were all willing to do whatever we had to in order to keep him happy—except, on Will's and my part, forsake our dreams—and he was happy, happy to have first one and then the other of his children back home with him.

"It is odd, Elizabeth," the old man said, for now I was Elizabeth again, the first week of Christmas holiday having passed, "is it not, that Will left for a week to stay with school friends just before your arrival? You two have always been so close—like brother and sister, really—I would have thought he would stay at least long enough to say hello."

What was really odd was having to get used to a corset again after so long without one. The dratted thing was driving me mad! Although it *was* nice not to have to bind my breasts for a week. And it was really nice that, as rare luck would have it, my week as Bet coincided with my monthly bleeding, so that for one month I would not have to contrive anything to do about *that.* On the other hand—there were so many other hands now!—it was all I could do to keep myself from striding manfully across rooms. I'd grown rather used to striding.

"It is odd, sir," I allowed now, "but it is also not odd."

"How do you mean?"

"Perhaps Will told his school friends that he would arrive at a certain time, and perhaps, further, Will has now matured enough that little things like—oh, I don't know—*punctuality* have grown important to him?"

"That doesn't sound like Will at all."

I had to admit that it did not. Why, right at that moment, Will was probably late for whatever battle he was supposed to be fighting in or at least drumming during.

Still, I felt as though I had to defend Will's honor. Or was it my honor now? Sometimes, it was all so confusing.

"But didn't you notice any changes in Will during the week he was here?" I asked.

"Changes? What sorts of changes?"

"Well, it's just that, in his letters to me at least, he really does seem to have grown up quite a bit. All he ever talks about now are his lessons, how important they've become to him, how proud he wishes to make you. Did you see none of that while he was here?"

"I suppose I did, now that you mention it. In truth, you are right, and he seemed quite changed. Still, given how close you two always were, the fact that he could not wait even a single hour longer for your arrival, it is *odd* . . ."

Odd? I knew what was odd. During the week I'd been Will, it was odd for me to talk about myself—meaning Bet—in the third person to the old man, discuss the letters I'd had from "her" all about her new position as companion and how she was liking it. It was just as disorienting in the second week to be talking about the changes and achievements of "Will" at school when, in reality, I was talking about myself!

If things became any more confusing . . .

"It was wonderful having Elizabeth here again for a whole week," the old man said. "I had no idea until she left to become companion to that . . . *woman*"—he refused, in his resentment, to call the new employer by name—"how much I'd grown to depend on her presence in this house."

When I'd woken up that morning, having contrived the ruse of Bet returning to Mrs. Larwood's the previous evening, I hadn't known who I was supposed to be. Should I put on a dress? A suit?

"Yes," I said now, having figured out that I was Will once again and having donned the appropriate suit. "You probably miss how she used to read to you, using all those voices, and how she could complete a piece of mending for you better than any of the other maids." I realized I had been unsuccessful in masking the resentment in my voice about the sort of things I assumed the old man might miss Bet for, but he didn't appear to notice my tone or take offense at it.

Rather, he waved my words aside with a dismissive hand.

"I couldn't care less about any of that," he said. "I simply miss *her*. I miss the light and energy she used to bring to this old house. I miss hearing the two of you scheme and bicker between yourselves as you used to do." He paused. "And I still do not understand why you could not stay at least an extra hour so that you might see her before trotting off to be with your school friends, and I really do not understand why that . . . *woman* she is now companion to insisted that she had to return to her job at a most exact hour so that she could not be here to see you—"

Oh, no. Not that again. Hadn't we already been down this road?

"I know I can never read to you half so good as Bet can, Uncle," I said. He was like a dog with a bone on the topic of the timing of Will's and my—or do I mean my and Bet's?—comings and goings, and I sought to distract him. "But if you like, I can read to you for a while. We have been studying Shakespeare's *Twelfth Night* at school, and while I don't think I can accomplish Bet's feat of mimicking male actors who are themselves mimicking female characters, I think I can at least do a credible job with the male voices."

"I suppose," he said. "I suppose that might be mildly entertaining."

I had hardly completed the first few scenes when the old man gave a discontented sigh.

"You read passably," he said, "but it is not the same."

I wasn't sure if I should feel insulted that my reading as Will was judged inferior or proud that my talents as Bet were so highly prized.

Since I was dressed in my Will costume at the time, it was easy to opt for being offended. It was what the real Will would have done.

"Would you like me to get you more port, Uncle, before I continue?" I offered through gritted teeth.

"Very well," he allowed, "very well."

By the time I got to act 2, the old man was beginning to drowse, sometimes snoring noisily, in his chair. He was a little drunk too.

"Shall I help you up to bed?" I offered. "Or perhaps get some of the servants?"

"No, that is . . ." He waved a hand, nodded off for a moment, then roused again with a start. "I have wondered sometimes," he said, "if I have been unfair in my treatment of Elizabeth."

"I'm sure she does not think so," I reassured him.

"Yes, but she doesn't know . . . you know . . . that's right, you don't know . . ."

What was he talking about?

"What doesn't she know?" I asked him. I had no idea what he could be referring to, but I certainly was alert now. "What don't I know?"

But it didn't matter how I phrased the question, for he'd nodded off to sleep again, this time more soundly than before. And when he finally did wake, he was obviously so confused and disoriented—an old man who'd fallen asleep in his chair beside a dying fire—I did not have it in me to press him further.

CHAPTER *nine*

All anyone could talk about was the dance.

January 15, 18—

Dear Will,

It was bad enough your not warning me in advance about compulsory sports, BUT I WOULD THINK YOU MIGHT HAVE MENTIONED DANCES!!! Imagine my horror—no, my humiliation—when, upon returning to school for Lent half, having successfully impersonated you at home over the holiday, I was informed that there is to be a *dance* here in one month's time? As you well know, I have never even received any training that would enable me to dance as a girl, which is what I am, never mind to lead as a boy, which is what I am supposed to be. Now I ask you: How am I supposed to pull *this* off? I can assure you, memorizing all of Homer and reciting it while standing on one foot would be easier.

Oh, and my roommate. To have *him* witness my humiliation, not to mention the way he will tease me . . . But that is a story for another time.

It occurs to me that it has been quite some time since I received a letter from you. I certainly hope you are still alive. I need you to be alive, Will, SO I CAN KILL YOU MYSELF FOR NOT WARNING ME ABOUT SCHOOL DANCES!!!

Your loving sister in spirit,
Bet

All anyone could talk about was the dance.

It was as though the whole world had gone mad.

We were at dinner at Marchand Hall our first night back. Hamish, seated at the head of the table, had just announced the specific Saturday in February that Dr. Hunter had informed him would be the night of the dance.

"What dance?" I whispered to James, hoping none of the others heard me.

He looked surprised at my question. "Why, the annual winter ball," he whispered in return, although he needn't have bothered; all around us, the others were chattering so excitedly about Hamish's news, we might have shouted and still not been overheard. "The days are so short now, the nights so long. It breaks up the monotony of the dreary cold season, gives everyone something to look forward to, and, at least according to the masters, provides us with the opportunity to comport ourselves as gentlemen."

That last sounded as though he was quoting something direct from Dr. Hunter's mouth.

"I thought we were always supposed to comport ourselves as gentlemen," I said, adding, with a snort, "well, except for when we're treeing one another or beating each other up without anyone trying to stop it." I was puzzled. "How does this 'dance' thing work?" I said. "What—we all dance with each other?"

"You mean, the boys with the boys?" he countered.

I nodded.

He looked at me for a long moment. Then: "How many schools did you say you'd been at before?"

"Three," I said, then shook my head in self-correction. "I mean four."

"And at all these other schools, either you never had dances or you all danced with each other?"

"Well, of course at my other schools we had dances. I suppose I just didn't pay much attention to them, and so I was, er, wondering what the protocol might be here." I was blathering now. "You know, every school I've been at differs in some way, however small, from the others. Sometimes chapel services are longer. Sometimes the food is even worse. Sometimes my room is on a different floor. So I think you will find it only natural that I would wonder—"

"*Girls,* Will." James cut me off. "We dance with *girls.*"

"Girls?" I sat back so abruptly, I almost tipped over in my chair. "Where do we get *girls* from? Surely, we're not all going to take turns dancing with Dr. Hunter's wife and Mrs. Smithers, are we?"

There was that long stare again. "Those dances at those other schools you attended—how many schools was that, again? twelve? twenty?—they must have really been something."

I was beginning to resent his remarks.

"We *invite* the girls, Will."

"Oh!"

"The older boys, some have sweethearts already, so they invite them. The younger boys and those who have no sweethearts invite sisters or cousins."

"Oh, I see."

I became lost in thought, envisioning myself as Will Gardener trying to lead Hamish's sister around the dance floor. Of course I did not specifically know him to have a sister, but James had said the boys without sweethearts brought relatives, and since it was impossible to picture Hamish with a sweetheart, suddenly I couldn't stop myself from picturing a barely feminine version of that most detested of boys, all dead fish eyes and meatiness in a dress. I shuddered. She'd probably beat me up if I didn't lead properly. It was going to be awful, a nightmare.

"Tyler!" Hamish's voice barking at my roommate intruded upon my happy thoughts. I looked up to see Hamish jutting out his chin at James. "Who're you bringing?"

"No one," James said coolly.

"Figures." Hamish turned to me, another chin jut. "And what about you, Gardener? No girls for you either?"

"Actually," I said, straightening in my chair, "I do have someone to invite."

"You do?" James asked before Hamish got the chance to.

"Yes. My sister, as a matter of fact."

"*You* have a sister? But you never said—" James began.

"And you never asked. But I do have one, all the same."

"And does this sister I've never heard of have a name?" James wanted to know.

"Oh, yes. Her name is Elizabeth, although we all call her Bet." I paused. "She's my identical twin."

"*Identical* twin?" James cocked an eyebrow at me. "Is your sister, then, perhaps a brother?"

"What?"

"It's just that identical twins must be the same gender. So if your twin is identical, either your twin is a boy, or *you* are *a girl*."

"Of course I know that." I felt the blush heat my face all the way up to my hairline. "What I *meant* to say is that Bet and I look so much alike, we might as *well* be identical twins."

"Oh, I see now." James eyed me coolly.

Three hours later, in bed for the night, the room darkened all around us, James still hadn't gotten over his surprise.

"I can't believe you kept something like that from me! You have an entire twin and I'm only just learning this four months after meeting you?"

"Is there any other kind of twin except an *entire* one? Are you suggesting it's possible that I might have *half* a twin, or possibly three-quarters of one? And what do you think I should have done, held out my hand back in September and said, 'Hullo, name's Will Gardener, and oh, by the way, I have a twin sister'?"

"No, of course not." I could hear his exasperation even though I couldn't see his face. "But you might have said at some point—"

"Don't you have any siblings you've never told me about?"

"No. I'm an only child."

"Oh."

"I still say that's quite a secret—"

"No secret, James. I'm not keeping any secrets at all. It just never came up before." I paused. "But now it has."

All I knew was, if there had to be a dance, I was damned if I was going to dance all night with Hamish's no doubt awful sister. Instead, I would dance, at least once, I hoped, with James.

As myself.

It is one thing to decide that one will impersonate a boy and successfully carry out that impersonation for four months and counting. It is one thing to decide that even though one is supposed to be a boy, one will turn around and masquerade as a girl to dance at a ball. But once one has made that second decision, it is quite another thing to figure out how one will actually pull it off.

What was I going to wear?

When James asked me to go into town with him that Sunday, I declined, saying I had some studying to do. When he offered to stay behind with me to help me study—perhaps I needed him to quiz me?—I hurried him out of the room, saying that what I was really in dire need of was a buttery scone from Parsons' Tea Room, and could he please bring one back for me? Preferably not too soon, because I really did need to study in silence. Then I locked the door behind him.

Alone now, I used the key to unlock my wardrobe and then removed my trunk. My wig was still there, as was the dress Will had so presciently urged me to pack when I'd first set out for school. I'd worn both when I'd appeared as Bet at Grangefield Hall that second week of Christmas holiday. But looking at that dress now—the efficient skirt, the unspectacular shade of pale blue—I knew it was nothing I could wear to a ball. And even if I could get an excused leave from school to travel home, it wasn't as though I'd find anything more suitable in my wardrobe there. Everyone at school knew Will Gardener came from a wealthy family. It wouldn't do for his twin sister to appear wearing something dowdy.

What to do . . . what to do . . .

After hastily shoving the trunk back into the wardrobe and locking it again, I hurried along to Mrs. Smithers's rooms. True, she might say no to my request. But I had to at least try.

I hesitated just a moment before raising my fist and knocking boldly. When she answered, I entered the room and shut the door behind me.

"This is a surprise, Gardener," she said saucily. "Have you suffered another fencing mishap?"

"I need a dress," I said without preamble.

She laughed. "Well, that's one thing none of the other boys here have ever asked me for."

"I can imagine," I agreed. "Still, I need one."

"I don't think any of mine would fit you," she said, still laughing.

Mrs. Smithers was both shorter and stouter than I was, not to mention that she was given to wearing dull colors and rough materials that looked like they had had too much starch.

"No, of course not." I blushed. "What I was hoping was that you could go into town and purchase for me—I would give you the money, of course—some luxurious material, perhaps a satin or a silk, enough so that I could sew myself a gown. I can sew, you see, but I'd need a kit. Do you have one? And I can't go into town myself, for if any of the boys saw me returning with a package and then looked inside and wondered what the bolt of fabric was for . . ."

"Yes, I can see where that could present a problem," she said dryly.

I imagined that she was picturing the same thing I was: Hamish hurling me to the ground, going through my purchases, and then confiscating them; or worse, teasing me about my taste in girlish things; or worst of all, figuring out what was really going on.

"And why do you need to make yourself a luxurious gown, if I may be so bold as to ask?"

"Because I want to go to the dance," I said.

"But why can't you go as a boy? Won't it be risky going as a girl?"

Of course it would be risky. But everything I'd done for the past four months had been risky.

I took a deep breath before speaking. "I want to go as a girl, because I want to dance with a particular boy."

Mrs. Smithers rolled her eyes at this. "There's always a boy, isn't there?"

Despite her reservations, Mrs. Smithers did as I'd asked her. She went into town and returned with a bolt of silk fabric the color of jade. My fingers thrilled to the touch of it. Even at Grangefield Hall, where Paul Gardener had made sure I'd wanted for nothing, I'd never had anything so fine.

And so began my period of secret sewing.

I told James that I could no longer concentrate in our room in the evenings—too much noise going on in the hall, I claimed—and then each night I sneaked out to Mrs. Smithers's rooms, taking great care not to be seen, and we'd work together on my project. She may have been reluctant in the beginning, but once we were properly into the thing, she was as committed to it as she had been to ensuring that no speck of dust ever stopped for long on a desk or a bedpost. As for James, if he thought it was odd, my sudden and inexplicable inability to tolerate extraneous noise while studying—and where, he would no doubt wonder, would I find a noiseless place at the Betterman Academy?—well, he'd thought me odd from the beginning, so there was nothing new there.

The rest of January passed in a blur of measuring, cutting, stitching. Through it all, Mrs. Smithers kept me entertained with a steady stream of chatter.

"I wish I'd had the opportunity to go to a school like this when I was your age," she said as I cut out one side of a sleeve.

"Course, if I had been lucky enough to be at school, as you are, I wouldn't have risked it all just for one dance with some boy, and which boy did you say it was?" she wanted to know as I carefully picked out a hem, trying not to ruin the fabric. Silk was so hard to work with!

"And even if I was going to risk everything just for one dance with a boy," she said as I labored to get the neckline just right, "I'd certainly keep up with my studying."

Ah, studying!

Of course, I had originally come to the Betterman Academy for an education, and I still had every intention of getting one. So after my long evenings with Mrs. Smithers, I'd go back to the room I shared with James and open my books.

"You haven't studied enough for one night," he'd ask me, "wherever it is you go when you're not here?"

"Now that it's quiet on the floor," I'd say, "I really should study some more."

"Have I told you lately how odd you are?" he'd ask.

"Repeatedly," I'd reply.

One night, as he patiently waited for me to finish studying so that we could go to sleep, he interrupted my reading with a question.

"When your sister comes," he asked, "where will she be staying?"

"Staying?"

"Yes. You didn't imagine she'd sleep on the floor here with us, did you? Not that I wouldn't be happy to offer up my bed, but I'm fairly certain Dr. Hunter frowns on us having girls in our rooms." I nearly choked at that. "And I don't think all the girls that are coming would fit into Mrs. Smithers's rooms."

Why had he mentioned Mrs. Smithers? Did he suspect something?

"Where *do* the girls stay, then?" I countered.

"In town," he said, stifling a yawn. "They stay at inns in town."

"Then," I said with a smile, "that's what Elizabeth will do too."

And then it was February.

And then, finally, it was the day of the winter ball.

Mrs. Smithers had wondered how I was going to achieve the feat of being two people at once—Will Gardener and his twin, Elizabeth—but I'd already worked that out. As anticipation of the evening grew, I fought back my excitement. I faked many sneezes. And as night drew closer, I took to my bed.

Then I waited. I waited for James to change into his finery and depart, so that I could spring into action.

But all my waiting was in vain as I watched my roommate read, read, read, his form stretched out across his bed.

At last, in exasperation, I said, "Shouldn't you be getting ready?"

"For what?" he asked absently, not even bothering to look up.

"Why, for the ball, of course!"

"Oh. That." He turned a page. "No."

"No?"

"No. I never go to these things."

Never . . .

I half rose in my bed, forgetting that I was supposed to be mildly ill. "But why ever not?"

"Because they are hopelessly dull affairs. Someone always smuggles in alcohol, someone else always drinks too much and vomits, and two other someones always fight over some girl." He turned another page. "Might as well just stay in with a good book. I'd suggest you do the same, but you have that sister of yours to escort. Your *identical* twin, wasn't it?"

I ignored his sarcasm. I was too stunned. This wasn't how things were supposed to go! Then I thought about the fact that, as excited as everyone else was about the dance—it was true, even the slightest change in routine made the others happy in winter—James hadn't really spoken about it, save for that one conversation we'd had the first night Hamish gave us the date, and that time he'd asked me where my sister was staying. And, I thought now, James had said he wasn't inviting anyone. Did James perhaps not even like girls? But I couldn't let myself think that.

"But you have to go!" I practically shouted at him.

"No," he said calmly. "I am fairly certain I do not. A dance is not like chapel or compulsory sports. I think they will still graduate me to the next form in the end."

"But you have to go!" I insisted again.

At last he looked up. "Why?"

And here I commenced the greatest impersonation of a sick person I could come up with. I faked sneezes. I faked a coughing fit. I doubled over as though my stomach were killing me.

Originally, I'd planned on James getting ready and leaving the room first. Then, when I showed up to the dance later on as Bet, I'd explain that my brother had been too ill to come. But now I had to alter the plan a bit. After all my careful preparations, it would be awful to go to the dance and not have James there.

"Are you going to live?" James asked when I'd taken a break from coughing.

"Just barely," I gasped. "But that's why you have to go. You must be there to keep an eye on Bet for me, since I'm obviously too sick to do so myself."

I coughed some more, groaned in agony a little bit.

James eyed me shrewdly. "Is this like that previous illness of yours, where you'll be able to predict for me the exact moment of your full recovery?"

I ignored that remark. "Imagine if *you* had a sister. I know that you do not, but imagine if you did. Would *you* want her going unattended to a dance where there would be the likes of Hamish and Mercy?"

James swung his legs to the floor and made for his wardrobe.

"I'll need to hurry," he said. "Which of the inns is she staying at?"

"Which inn?"

"Yes, so I can call for her."

"Oh, you don't need to do that," I hurriedly said. "She and I already arranged that she will make her way here on her own, and we will simply meet at the dance."

James snorted as he pulled out a fine black tie to go with the suit he'd selected. "You're not exactly a chivalrous brother, are you?"

I relaxed back into the pillow, smiling widely, since with his back turned, he couldn't see my expression.

"No, I guess not," I admitted. "That's where you come in."

Then, for good measure, I coughed again.

You think you have planned for everything, but there is always one small detail you haven't accounted for, one small thing that trips you up.

I had no shoes.

"I can't wear my boots with this gown!" I was practically hysterical as I stood in my jade dress before Mrs. Smithers, staring down at my feet.

"No," she observed ruefully, "you can't, nor do I have anything better to lend you. At least your hair looks nice."

Small comfort, that. Yes, it felt good to have long hair again, even if it was only a wig. That and the dress gave me a rare feeling of being beautiful, although I'd had to take great care to secure the wig with extra pins, worrying that if James did dance with me, it might be a reel, and what if the wig flew off?

But what good did feeling beautiful in my wig and dress do me now? I was dejected, nearly inconsolable. To have come so far only to have my dream frustrated for want of the proper shoes.

"I know!" she said, brightening as she snapped her fingers. "You wait here!"

And she was gone.

I waited impatiently for her return, wondering where she'd raced off to. There wasn't enough time for her to go into town, buy shoes, and come back before the dance started. And even if there had been, the shops wouldn't be open this late.

After what seemed an eternity, but which the ticking clock told me was only ten minutes, she returned.

But she wasn't alone.

As she stole into the room, I saw with horror that the person accompanying her was Dr. Hunter's wife.

"Oh no!" I cried at Mrs. Smithers. "What have you done?"

But she just smiled, and before she could say anything, Mrs. Hunter pulled a pair of pretty gold dancing slippers from behind her back.

"They may be too big," she said in an elegant voice. Then she added with a laugh, "Dr. Hunter has often commented on my large feet."

I was stunned. "You're helping me?"

"Of course," she said, taken aback. "We women need to stick together, don't we?"

Then, with no care for her own pretty gown, she knelt down before me to place the slippers on my feet. Since I was relatively tall and large of feet myself, the shoes fit perfectly.

Mrs. Smithers beamed. "It pays to know who to trust in life, don't it?"

"There," Mrs. Hunter said, straightening up. "You look wonderful, dear."

"I still don't understand," I said.

"I believe in education. And I wish I had had a proper one—maybe then Dr. Hunter would talk to me about something other than my feet! And I believe in romance. Now then." She clapped her pretty hands together. "How are we going to get you out of Proctor Hall with no one seeing you?"

"That one's easy," Mrs. Smithers said. "We've already worked it out." She disappeared from the room, then returned with two sheets that had been securely knotted together. Mrs. Smithers's rooms were at the back side of Proctor Hall; the windows opened on a walkway that hardly anyone used.

"I see," Mrs. Hunter said, looking impressed. "Well then . . ."

I swung my legs over the window ledge, grabbed on tight to the end of the sheet, and they lowered me down.

"Whoever he is," Mrs. Smithers called after me softly, "I hope he's worth it."

As I hurried through the commons area, making my way toward Marchand Hall, I thought about what Mrs. Smithers had said. I'd wanted an education, and now here I was, risking it all for a boy. Was James worth it? But then I wondered, Why did I have to choose? Why, if I wanted, could I not have both? At least for one night.

I lifted my skirts slightly so I wouldn't trip over them in the unfamiliar shoes—boots were really so much more comfortable to walk in!—and hurried on.

Marchand Hall didn't look at all like it usually did. For one thing, there were not five hundred boys chattering loudly as they threw dinner rolls at one another's heads. For another, the tables we usually dined at had been removed, leaving the space wide open for dancing, which was already going on to the accompaniment of the waltzes provided by musicians in one corner. Along the far wall, where Dr. Hunter usually sat, a table had been set up for refreshments. And there was one other big difference: there were a lot of young ladies in the room.

And yes, not one but *two* of those young ladies were meaty and bore a striking resemblance to Hamish! It was amazing to think that something I had imagined had some resemblance to reality.

After all my planning, now that I was here I was suddenly nervous. Yes, I was here as Will Gardener's sister. But I wasn't supposed to have met anyone before. So I couldn't very well approach Little, who was standing nervously by the refreshments table. And I certainly didn't want to approach Hamish and Mercy, who appeared to be making nuisances of themselves around one girl while Hamish's sisters hovered nearby. And I certainly, absolutely could not approach James, who looked heartachingly handsome and who was alone in another corner, scanning the room for something. All I could do was stand in my own corner, nervously tapping my foot to the music, a gay smile plastered on my face as though I were having the time of my life, trying to act as though I had a companion who had merely been called away for a moment but who would soon return.

"Miss Gardener?"

I almost jumped at the sound of James's voice. Up close, I saw, he was even more handsome than he'd been from across the room.

"Yes?" I forced my tone to sound as though I had no clue as to who he might be. With horror, I realized I'd used my Will voice and prayed James hadn't noticed it in that one syllable.

"I am James Tyler," he said, "your brother's roommate. He asked me if I would look out for you this evening since he has fallen ill."

"I know," I said, making sure to sound like a girl this time. "He had a message sent to the inn."

Before we could speak any further, we were interrupted by Hamish, who had apparently shaken off his sisters for the time being. "You must be Gardener's twin!" he said. "I'd know that face anywhere."

"The resemblance is remarkable," James observed.

"I must say, though," Hamish said, "the face looks a lot better on you than it does on your brother." He held out his arms. "Care for a dance?"

I couldn't think of anything I would care to do less.

"She doesn't want to dance with you," Mercy said, joining us, arms outstretched. "I'm sure she'd rather dance with me."

And now I *could* think of something I'd care to do less. Really, the idea of being waltzed around the room by either of them was too unbearable.

"I am afraid I will have to decline both invitations," I forced myself to say sweetly. "For with two of you to choose from, how can I possibly decide?"

"You should have waited till after I'd had my turn." Hamish clouted his friend on the shoulder.

Mercy's hand moved to rub the spot where he'd been hit. "How was I supposed to know?"

As they argued their way over to another girl, James turned to me.

"You handled that very well, Miss Gardener. In fact, I don't think your own brother could have managed any better."

"Oh, really?" I laughed. "You mean Will regularly has to fend off unwelcome dancing partners too?"

James studied me before speaking. "You're very like him, you know."

"Well, we are twins, after all."

"Obviously," he said. "But I don't mean just that. There's something . . ."

"Are you ready for a dance now?" Hamish was back, this time without Mercy.

"Not quite." I forced the smile to remain on my face until he departed.

A moment later, I saw one of Hamish's sisters tap him insistently on the shoulder. Grudgingly, he held his arms out for a dance. Then the other sister tapped insistently on Mercy's shoulder, and he too consented with little grace. I watched for a time as the girls led Hamish and Mercy around the room. It was rather fun seeing Hamish and Mercy get pushed around for once, particularly by a pair of girls.

"You know," James said, "it is a dance. You're supposed to dance with people."

Yes, I did know that. But there was only one person there I wanted to dance with. Really, it was the only reason I had come.

"Perhaps," I said, realizing even as I spoke that it was the most flirtatious thing I'd ever said in my life, "I'm just waiting for the right person to ask."

"Well, until that happens, will I do? At the very least, it will keep Hamish and Mercy away from you for a time."

How could a girl refuse an offer like that?

I allowed him to tuck my hand into the crook of his elbow, lead me out onto the floor. I felt him take one of my hands in his, felt him place the other hand at my waist.

In my whole life, no one had ever touched me like that.

I wanted to close my eyes and give in to the moment, but I couldn't do that. Supposedly, I had known him for only a few minutes. He would think I was insane. So instead:

"Do you know how to dance, Mr. Tyler?"

"I think I can manage a waltz without doing you any bodily harm," he said, launching us.

"That makes one of us, then," I said, attempting to follow his lead.

"You don't dance?"

"Not regularly, no," I said, keeping my eyes on my feet, "although I appear to be doing so now."

"I thought all girls liked to dance."

It was a while before I responded. I was finding it challenging to dance and talk at the same time.

"I did not say I didn't like to," I finally said, looking up. "I said it wasn't an activity I regularly engaged in. And anyway, how can you assume all girls like to do one thing? Do all boys like to do any one particular thing?"

"You really are a lot like your brother."

"I believe you've said that already. So, what of that brother of mine? You live together. Do you like him?"

He stopped dancing and drew away a bit.

Oh no, I thought. What a stupid question to ask. Now he would tell me that he didn't like Will, and by doing so, he would be saying that he didn't like me.

"Well," he said, considering, "I don't know as I've ever thought of your brother in terms of *liking.* He is intelligent and funny, and yet there's a certain nobility about him. It's as though questions of honor and integrity matter to him in a way that they don't matter to anyone else here, certainly not the masters. I can no longer remember what it was like here before your brother came, and I certainly can't imagine what it would be like if he were gone." He shrugged, looking stunned at his admission. "I suppose Will Gardener is the best friend I've ever had."

I was feeling all sorts of emotions then: stunned, thrilled, and not a little jealous. Stunned, because I had known James was fond of me, at least compared to how he felt about the likes of Hamish and Mercy, but I hadn't known it was to such an extent; thrilled, because of that very fondness; and jealous, because it had been possible for me to grow close to James only as Will Gardener. I could never have gotten so close to him if he had met me as Bet, the maid's daughter. What a peculiar world it was, never mind how much more peculiar I had made it.

"You look unhappy," James said.

"I'm sorry?"

"If hearing that I regard your brother as my best friend makes you unhappy," he said, forcing a laugh, "I can certainly pretend he is my mortal enemy."

And now here was another peculiar feature. Had I been James's friend Will right then, I knew James would never be so solicitous about my mood. There was something tender and protective about his behavior, in contrast with the bluff fraternal nature of his friendship with Will. And, I realized now, he would never have confessed to Will what he had just told me.

"It is all right," I said with feigned hauteur that I made sure to moderate with a bright smile. "I rather like that you like my brother. You may go on doing so."

"Are you ready to dance now?" Oh God. Hamish again. Apparently, he'd emancipated himself from his sister.

"Much as I would like to," I said, "I'm afraid I see someone I promised my brother I would dance with this evening."

"Who?" Hamish was outraged.

I jutted my chin toward a boy who was shuffling his feet around the refreshments table while Stephens looked on from the other side.

"Little?" Hamish was more outraged yet.

"I thought my brother said his name was Christopher Warren," I said coolly. "Will described him to me right down to that shock of red hair and told me he had a sterling character. Now, if you will excuse me . . ."

I made my way straight over to a stunned Little, feeling James and Hamish staring after me. I was sure James looked amused while Hamish was practically apoplectic that I'd turned him down in favor of Little. As for Little, so what if he crippled my toes with stepping on them as we each attempted to lead the other around the dance floor? It was worth it to catch that look on Hamish's face every time I spun around.

After Little and I were finished, I made my way back to James.

"That was a nice thing you did for Little," James said. "You know, it's probably the only dance he'll ever get in his entire career here."

I waved off what he clearly intended as a compliment.

"Would you care to dance with me again?" he offered.

"No, thank you." I laughed. "Christopher stepped on my toes so many times, I think I'm done dancing for the night."

"I'm sorry about that," he said, nodding at my feet.

"Don't be." I shrugged. "It was well worth it."

"Would you like to sit down? Can I get you some refreshments?"

"I think," I said, "that I'd just like to stand here and watch, if you don't mind."

And really, it was all I wanted right then.

It was funny. I'd come to the winter ball with my only desire being to dance with James, and yet, after just one brief dance, I had refused a second. In part, that refusal was because it had been almost too much, feeling his hand take mine, feeling his other hand against my waist—I'd been touched so few times in my life, any physical contact was shocking. But a far bigger part was the realization that sometimes we want things, and then when we get them, we see that what we really want is something else. And all I truly wanted in that moment was just what I had: to be standing there, a girl, next to a boy I liked so much, watching the world dance by.

"Very well," James said.

So that's what we did.

As it began to grow late, I asked James if we might step outside for a moment.

"It's February," he said.

"Not June?"

"It'll be cold," he said.

"It'll feel good."

I walked, and James followed, until we were far away from the golden lights of Marchand Hall, and then I spun around.

"Would you like to kiss me?" I asked.

"Would I . . . You're Will's sister!"

"Yes, I do know that. Would you like to kiss me?"

I didn't care how bold or forward I sounded. I wanted that kiss. I knew that if everything went according to my original plan, if I succeeded in finishing out my time at the Betterman Academy as Will Gardener, I'd never get another chance like this.

"I can't—" he started to say.

But I didn't let him finish.

Stepping into the space that separated us, I rose on my toes and tilted my head up, touching my lips to his.

Then, before he could say anything, I settled back on my feet, raised my skirts slightly, and took off running across the commons area.

"Where are you going?" he shouted after me.

"I'll be late for my carriage!" I shouted back. I could hear the joy in my voice even as I heard the chapel clock strike the hour.

It struck me then that I was like a character from a story written back in 1697, Charles Perrault's Cinderella, only in my case, I'd been able to hold on to both slippers, and they weren't made of glass.

"I'll walk you," James called out. He began to run.

"No!" I shouted cheerfully but in a voice that brooked no argument. "You stay there! Enjoy the dance!" I ran some more, turned one last time to see him still standing there. "Thank you!" I shouted.

A few pebbles thrown carefully at Mrs. Smithers's window was enough to make her open up for me, and I scampered back up the sheets as she and Mrs. Hunter pulled from the other end.

"Was it everything you hoped it would be?" Mrs. Smithers asked as I all but tumbled into the room.

"It'll have to be," I said. "It'll have to be enough."

"Did you have a good time?" I asked my roommate from my position in bed, sheets pulled up to my chin.

"You know, I did," he said, sounding surprised. He removed his tie.

"And what of my sister?" I couldn't help but ask. "What did you think of her?"

He was silent for a long moment. Then: "She's as odd as you are, isn't she?"

CHAPTER *ten*

February 18, 18—

Dear Will,

Well, I have really put my foot in it. I have gone and fallen in love for the first time, and with my own roommate, no less! I can hear you laughing at me now: "This is a fine kettle of fish, Bet! You say you want to impersonate a boy—me; you say you want to go to all this trouble so you can obtain a proper education. And what happens at the end of the day? You fall in love! That is so like a girl—and *that* is why education is wasted on girls! Now what, pray tell, do you plan to do? After all, your first plan has worked out so well!"

Fine. Laugh all you want to. But I can assure you, it is not funny. I can further assure you, if you have never had such feelings yourself, that I have come to learn that one does not choose whom one falls in love with. Yes, it would have been nice if I could have waited until after my original plan had been successfully executed here at the Betterman Academy. Yes, it would have been nice if the object of my (great) affections had turned out to be someone suitable, someone I met after all this, someone whom I had not met under false pretenses. And preferably someone of my own station, since what boy whose family can afford to send him away to school would ever possibly grow warm feelings for the maid's daughter? But since, as I say, one has no choice in these matters of love, it is useless to talk about what "would have been nice."

Oh, Will. I am heartsick, and in every way imaginable. I am heartsick because I am in love. I am heartsick because the object of that love has no knowledge of my feelings, nor can he ever! For I have determined that the only possible action to take is no action; I shall continue my quest to get an education until it is completed. And so I will put my feelings aside, push them down as though they never existed, and I will redouble my efforts in my lessons until I achieve what now seems impossible: forgetting I ever had those feelings in the first place.

Oh, Will! I wish you were here! Or I wish, at the very least, that you would write me back, even if you laugh at me throughout your letter, for then I would know that you are well. Which I do not know, since it has been so very long since I have had any letters from you.

Please, write and tell me you are well. Please, write and tell me what a foolish little idiot I have been and how stupid it is of me to have allowed my heart to become so engaged.

Your sister in spirit,
Bet

❦

The Sunday morning after the winter ball found me up early and at my desk, having resolved to attack my studies with renewed vigor.

James, on the other hand, woke up angry.

"I can't believe this!" he said, sitting bolt upright in bed and blinking against the glare of all the lamps I'd lit and the light streaming through the window's open shutters. "It's bad enough to have a roommate who insists on going to sleep in pitch darkness so that if I must rise in the middle of the night, I practically kill myself merely attempting to cross my own room. But now my insane roommate has to insist on so much light on Sunday morning, and so early, when the rest of the sane world is still sleeping?"

I resented that remark about my sanity. Or lack thereof.

I looked up from my studies just long enough to see a confused look cross his face.

"And was that *birds* I heard chirping?" he went on. "*Birds* chirping in *England* in the middle of *February?*" He paused, cocked an ear. "Funny, I don't hear anything now." Another pause, followed by an accusing: "It was *you,* wasn't it? You were *whistling while you worked,* weren't you?"

I felt the blush coloring my cheeks, for more reasons than one.

"Good morning, James," I said, forcing myself to look at him, forcing a normal tone into my voice as if nothing had changed between us in the past day and night because as far as he knew, it hadn't. "I trust you slept well after the dance?"

"Hey!" he said, ignoring my polite query. "You're well again! You're not coughing and sneezing as if you're dying, and you're up early, whistling like a bird!"

"Yes, well, I—"

"I knew it. I knew it! I knew yesterday, when you claimed to be so ill, that you would make a speedy and miraculous recovery from your deathbed, just like you did the last time. So tell me, what was *that* all about?"

He didn't wait for me to answer, which was good, since I didn't have an answer; certainly not one I was willing to share.

"I know!" He snapped his fingers at me so abruptly I flinched a little in my seat. "You were worried that if you went with Bet, none of the other boys would dance with her, and you just wanted her to have a good time."

"How did you guess?"

"Well, I've never been a brother, but I have read about them in books. So I know that sometimes they undervalue their sisters, think that no one will want to dance with them, so I'm guessing you figured that if you asked me to look out for her, of course I wouldn't allow her to have a bad time."

"Yes, well, I—"

"But don't you see, Will? You needn't have gone to so much bother."

"I needn't?"

"No, of course not. A girl like Bet would be fine no matter who was or wasn't with her."

"She would?"

"Of course!"

"But, er . . . why?"

"Because she's pretty."

"Well, I'm sure she would love to receive such a compliment. You know, if she were here."

"But it's more than that."

"More than pretty?"

"Oh, yes. You may not see it, since you're her brother, Will. But your sister is kind and intelligent and funny. And special."

I confess it without qualm. When I heard James say that about Bet, I had one reaction, even though I couldn't let him see it:

Swoon!

Oh, this was worse than worse.

As Bet, I liked James, but could not confess that liking, while James could do nothing about his liking for Bet.

"Do you think your sister might visit again this term?" he asked tentatively one night while we were studying.

"No," I said. "She is kept quite busy at home. Besides which, have you not seen the snow on the ground lately? I would think that even Father Christmas would be hard-pressed to get through."

"Perhaps when the spring arrives . . . ?"

"No!" I practically shouted at him. "No." I forced a more reasonable tone into my voice. "You must realize that you are placing me in a most awkward position here."

"And how is that?"

"Well." It was all I could do not to squirm in my seat from discomfort. "It is obvious to me that you fancy yourself fond of, er, *Bet.*"

"I never said—"

"And I can certainly understand that. As you have said, she is pretty and kind and intelligent and funny and—what was that other word you used?"

"Special."

"Of course. *Special.* But I, as you well know, am her brother. I am also, as you well know, your roommate. So I don't see how you can possibly expect—"

"I never said anything about fondness."

"No, but—"

"I never said *anything* that should cause you to dither on so."

"No, of course not, but—"

"All I asked,"—James half rose out of his seat as he shouted at me—*"was if she might be visiting again this term!"*

"Oh. Well then, the answer would be no. I'm afraid I do not think that will happen."

I don't know how James felt, but this was starting to exhaust me.

Honestly, it was easier, not to mention safer, to put my nose to the grindstone and just study.

Study, study, study.

Two weeks after the dance, March on the horizon, it was still all anybody could talk about. We were all at dinner, Marchand Hall ringing with the sound of five hundred boys eating, and Stephens was regaling us with his own memories of the night.

Stephens was the boy who'd told Hamish and Mercy where Little and I were the day they'd surprised us fishing by the river. Stephens, a spotty-skinned boy with dirty hair who'd been held back more than once for failing to show the intelligence to advance to the next form, had originally struck me as the sort who wasn't so much stupid as scheming, always angling for better position in the pecking order. If that meant doing things that might result in other boys' harm, like informing on Little and me, so be it.

Early on, I'd gotten the impression that all Stephens's angling was in the hopes of displacing Mercy as second to Hamish; no one could displace Hamish. In recent days, that impression had changed. Now I thought that Stephens accepted that Mercy's ability to supply Hamish with beer, not to mention Mercy's skill at providing Hamish with the optimum level of sycophancy, meant that Mercy would never be supplanted. The hierarchy of our little universe at Betterman was too firmly in position. Nothing would alter it now. I believed that Stephens resented this more than most, and for some time he'd been seizing every opportunity to throw what little daggers he had Hamish's way.

"Gardener's sister really was something!" Stephens said to the table at large.

To my surprise, there was a chorus of approving murmurs. Who would have ever guessed I'd be such a success with so many? But then, the night of the dance, I'd really only had eyes for James, so perhaps

I'd failed to notice some of the other things that were going on around me.

"Yes, she really was," Stephens went on enthusiastically when it became apparent that the others were going to do no more than murmur in reply. "So pretty. And so sharp, by all accounts."

I must say, I did feel rather flattered on my own behalf.

"And what a fine dancer!" Stephens said with awe in his voice, as though the girl he was talking about had somehow invented dancing. "Wouldn't you say so, Tyler?" he said, addressing James.

"She was adequate," James allowed, refusing to look up from his meal.

At first I was offended at this—adequate?—but then I realized from the dejected slope of James's shoulders that he was no doubt still smarting from the discussion we'd had about when Bet might or might not make another appearance.

"I'd say she was more than adequate," Stephens said. He turned to Little. "Wouldn't you say so, Little? Why, I was sure I saw you spin her around the room at least once."

"It was . . . it was . . . it was the time of my life," he finally hiccupped out. Then he blushed in my direction. "I hope I haven't offended you, Will."

"No offense taken," I reassured him.

"The time of your life," Stephens echoed thoughtfully. "Yes, I could see how someone could feel that way about such a girl. Wouldn't you say so, Hamish?"

Hamish scowled.

"Oh, that's right. You wouldn't know, would you?" Stephens spoke the words with such oversweetness he might have been a nasty girl about to steal her grandmother's last tart. "Gardener's sister refused to dance with you."

Hamish scowled some more, but Stephens wouldn't leave it alone.

"Gardener's sister even danced with Little—with *Little!*—but she refused to dance with you."

That's when Hamish lunged at Stephens's neck.

❦

Once you have heard a thing, no matter how hard you might try to forget it, it is impossible to *un*hear it. And so it was with the words James had spoken on the night of the dance: he regarded me—*Will*—as his best friend. It was therefore now impossible for me to think of myself in any other way.

In the aftermath of Hamish's lunging for Stephens's neck at dinner, James was shaken.

"I don't see how," he said, "the masters can chalk this up to yet another instance of 'boyish high jinks'!"

"You know how things are around here," I said softly. "It doesn't do to expect it ever to be any different. And as Little always points out, there's no point in running from it."

"But did you see the marks on Stephens's neck?"

Of course I had seen them. We all had.

"Come on," I said. "At least we tried."

This was true. For once not content to sit idly by and watch as one of our number was physically abused, James and I, as though thinking with one mind, had attempted to restrain Hamish. Not that it had done much good. So angry was he at Stephens, Hamish had had the strength of three boys, shrugging off our efforts as he'd proceeded to throttle Stephens.

"Come on," I said again.

And then I did something I should never have done, made a mistake far graver than thinking I could fight Hamish. Wanting to make James feel better—not even sure in the moment if I was thinking of myself as Will, the roommate James regarded as his best friend, or as Bet, the girl who liked James—I reached out and covered his hand with mine.

"What are you doing?" He snatched his hand back as though I'd burned him.

"I'm, I'm sorry," I stammered. "I don't know what I was thinking."

"I should think not," he said hotly. And then, for the second time in our acquaintance, in our *friendship,* he stormed from the room.

I stood there, alone, confused.

I no longer knew exactly what I felt at any given moment, no longer knew who I was or who I was supposed to be.

❦

Worse had come to even worse, and now, if at all possible, it had come to worst.

I spent my days—and even more, my nights—in a constant state of confusion, unsure how to act around James. These feelings I had for him, they were like nothing I had ever experienced before in my life. It was as though my brain was as confusingly labyrinthine as the lair of the Minotaur; my heart, no better. And my body! It was bad enough that my hand appeared to have a persistent memory of what it felt like to have James hold it during that short dance we'd shared together. It was bad enough that the first thing I thought of upon waking in the morning and the last thing I thought of before falling asleep was what it had felt like to briefly—oh, too briefly—press my lips to his. But now my whole body, places that I'd never expected could feel wanting, tilted in his direction, as if he were a star pulling me into his orbit.

Unable to act on these longings, in my frustration I turned to other physical activity.

I returned to fencing.

"En garde!" I screamed at Hamish.

He all but laughed in my face. After our last fencing incident, and Mrs. Smithers's subsequent request that I be excused from compulsory sports for a while, I'd been careful to avoid all physical contests. The most I would do, when it was still warm enough and before the earth became covered with snow, was run around on the cricket field like a lunatic, as far away from the action as I could get.

But I was ready for contact now.

"Are you sure you want to try this again?" Hamish stood there, his guard down, laughing.

"En garde!" I cried again, this time thrusting at him.

"Hey, you're serious!" Late, too late, he brought up his foil to parry my thrust.

But he was moving far too slow, or perhaps he still believed he could beat me with one meaty hand tied behind his back.

I took the hilt of my foil in both fists, gripped it as though it were an ax, and swung at his weapon with everything that was in me. My force ripped it from his hand. Keeping my eye on my target, I had the sense of his now useless weapon flying benignly over our heads.

"Take that!" I said, thrusting my weapon at him one-handed now and causing him to take a step backward. "That is for Stephens, even if he doesn't totally deserve to be revenged."

Was that a glimmering of fear I saw in Hamish's eyes?

"Take that!" I said, thrusting again, causing him to take another stumbling step backward. "That is for Little."

Now he looked as though he thought he was dealing with a lunatic. Well, let him think so.

"Take that!" I thrust, my most powerful thrust yet. "That is for the rest of us."

I thrust and I thrust until I had backed him against the wall. Once he was there, I held the ball-covered point of the foil to his neck as I ripped off my fencing mask.

"You are just lucky," I said with a smile, "that the point has that little ball on it, or you would be dead right now."

If I thought Hamish hated me before, that was nothing compared with what I saw in his eyes now.

But oh, it had been worth it.

Oh, this was worse than the worst.

"I can't believe you went after Hamish like that!" James said.

"I know." I rubbed my wrist. It was sore from swinging the foil so hard. "It was great, wasn't it?"

"Great? It was bloody awful!"

Oh.

"You were like one of them," he said.

I saw then that he was right. After the time Hamish had mercilessly beat me while fencing, I'd told myself that it would be wrong to allow myself to become like Little, cowering in fear before bullies. I'd wanted revenge on Hamish, had exacted out small revenges, like putting vinegar in his beer or dousing him with water, and I obviously still thirsted for revenge, given how I'd attacked him a short time ago. But what I hadn't seen after that original beating was that if it was wrong for me to become like Little, it was just as wrong to become like Hamish, throwing the first blow for the sheer fun of it, no matter what the provocation or even if there had been any at all. It made me think of Will and his desire to go to war, the desire of so many boys to go to war, and I wanted no part of it.

"You are—" I started to say but was cut off.

"Ever since that dance," he went on, "which you didn't even bother going to, I might add, you've been different."

"Different? How so?"

"It's like you're not the same Will that I knew. Or it's like part of you is the same, but part of you is someone I don't remember meeting."

"Maybe it's just that we're finally getting to know one another."

"No, it's not that, I don't think. I don't know what it—"

Just as I'd done instinctively on another occasion, I reached out and covered his hand with mine.

"That!" he said, flushing furiously as he wrenched his hand away from me, taking a step backward at the same time. "*That's* something you never used to do!"

I didn't know what to say, what to do.

"You've just been behaving so strangely," he said, "like this . . . this . . . this *touching* thing." He rubbed his hand, as though he were physically wounded. "And sometimes when I see your face, in particular when you whipped off your fencing mask, I see *her.* It is most . . . *disconcerting.*" He paused, then surprised me by laughing, but it wasn't a happy sound. "I know now! The real reason you faked illness to avoid the dance. It's because you're scared of girls, isn't it? Or at least, you don't like them as such."

"James."

If you are lucky, every now and then you are granted a moment of clarity. And in that moment, I saw past my own confusion into a window on James's confusion. He liked Will—his best friend—but he liked Will's sister in a different way. And yet with Bet nowhere around, he had found himself increasingly attracted to his friend, and he was disturbed by this. I wished I could explain to him that what I was seeing now was something that had never occurred to me before: that we like, even love, those whom we have feelings for because of who they are as individuals, and not because of some external trappings. James had liked and admired Will before the advent of Will's sister—Will's sister, who looked pretty in jade, who may not have been a good dancer but who was sportingly game, and who was kind to Little. And he liked Will's sister for what he no doubt thought were entirely different reasons than he liked her brother, not knowing they were the same person. Would he still like her once he learned the truth behind what she'd done?

I had no idea. All I knew was that he was in agony and I had to do something about it. Ever since the winter ball, we had been circling each other in a strange dance. It was time to put an end to that now.

"James." I spoke his name in as steady a voice as I could, even as my heart hammered within my chest.

"Yes?" he said, a trifle nervously. "I believe you've said my name once already."

"It has been a long day," I said slowly, "and we are tired."

"Yes," he agreed.

"Perhaps we should just go to sleep and continue this in the morning?"

Without saying another word to me, he crossed to his wardrobe and got his things out. For once, I turned my back to him as he changed, much as I enjoyed my glimpses of his naked body.

"Shall I shut these for you?" he said. I turned to see him standing at the window, pushing it up so he could get at the shutters outside.

"Not tonight," I said quietly. "Why don't you leave them open?"

"Oh." I heard the surprise in his voice. Why, he must have been wondering, was this night different than the ones that had gone before?

Without another word, he climbed into his bed.

It was then I made my own preparations. Pulling from my pocket the key I always kept there, I unlocked my wardrobe, removed my nightshirt and one other item, and shut the door again. Then, with my back to James, I removed my jacket, my waistcoat, my tie, my shirt. Almost naked to the waist now, I began slowly unwinding the length of cloth that bound my breasts.

"What . . . ?" I heard the confusion in his voice.

Trousers still on, I lifted up the nightshirt and pulled it on over my head, feeling it drift down over my body. Only then did I remove my trousers. And finally, at last, I donned the other item I had extracted from the wardrobe: my wig.

The fear was on me again, that familiar fear of exposure. It was a huge risk I was taking. What if he did not feel about me as I felt about him? What if I was wrong and he really did prefer boys, and, seeing that I was a girl, he became repulsed and turned me in? But I no longer cared about the risk. No, that is not true. Of course I still cared about it, but I cared more about him, putting him out of his misery of confusion. And for once, just once, I wanted to be seen for who I really was, to be seen by *him.*

Slowly, I turned around.

"What?" James was out of the bed so fast he nearly stumbled at my feet. *"Who . . . ?"*

"Bet," I said as calmly as I could. "I have always been Bet."

"Not Will?" he asked wonderingly.

"Never Will."

As though his body knew things his mind did not, he reached a hand toward my face and touched my cheek with the lightest feather touch, as though my skin were an exhibit in a museum.

It took all the bravery I had left in me to ask one final question: "Would you like to kiss me?"

❦

One night not long after, as James and I studied in our room, pretending not to be as aware of each other as we were, a knock came at our door. A loud knock.

Being closer, I opened the door, and Dr. Hunter sailed through, his black robe billowing behind him. I swear, Dr. Hunter always entered a room like that. It was as though he arrived with his own wind.

"Gardener," he announced, "I wish to speak with you a moment in private." He turned to James and instructed, "If you would excuse us, Tyler."

James cast a look of concern in my direction as he slowly made for the door, but that was all he could do. He couldn't very well refuse the headmaster, could he?

"If you could perhaps move just a trifle faster, Tyler," Dr. Hunter suggested. "I did say it would only be a moment, but I'd just as soon that moment happen this evening and not have you take so long in exiting that I'm still here in the morning waiting for it."

Once James was gone, Dr. Hunter shut the door with a decisive click before whirling on me.

"You may not have been aware of it, Gardener, but ever since you first arrived here, I have been keeping a close eye on you."

Oh no, I thought.

"First, there was the matter of your dismal records from your previous schools. Honestly, Gardener, even MacPherson and Mercy have been sent down only three times. But really, four? Even you must realize how excessive a number that is. And from a headmaster's standpoint, it is hardly reassuring."

Oh no, I thought again. *Here it comes.*

"Then there was the matter of your thinking it was acceptable to make a complaint to me about your fellow students. That sort of thing says a lot about a . . . *boy's* character. And now there is . . . *this*—this thing that has happened that has caused me to rethink everything I thought about you."

Here it comes, I thought. *I knew it was a mistake for Mrs. Smithers to trust my secret to Mrs. Hunter on the night of the winter ball! She must have been unable to keep it from her husband—or perhaps she felt that an omission of the truth was the same as the commission of a lie; it preyed on her conscience too much, and finally she could stand it no longer, just as I was no longer able to keep the truth from James? Whatever the case, here it comes,* I thought, surprised in that part of what I felt was relief.

". . . first in your class."

"What? Excuse me, Dr. Hunter, but what did you just say?"

"Gardener! Were you *woolgathering* as I was speaking to you?" He didn't wait for an answer, instead going on with no small degree of annoyance. "I *said:* Imagine my surprise when, given my previous reservations about you, Mr. Winter and all the other masters informed me that you have applied yourself so thoroughly here at Betterman that you are now first in your class."

"First in my class?"

"Yes, it means that of all the boys in your form, your ranking exceeds everyone else's. As a matter of fact, according to your masters, it far exceeds everyone else's."

When I remained standing there, struck dumb, Dr. Hunter grew visibly impatient. "Honestly, Gardener," he said disgustedly, reaching for the door, "I am beginning to wonder if you can possibly be as intelligent as they all claim you are!"

The door clicked shut behind him.

First in my class!

CHAPTER *eleven*

"First in your class! First in *our* class!"

James was thrilled at my accomplishment, and I was thrilled that he was thrilled.

"I don't believe that I ever imagined," James went on, "in the days when I envisioned myself falling in love, that the object of my love would turn out to be more intelligent than I am, at least according to the masters, or that when we move up to the next form she'd be ahead of me."

The next form . . . I hadn't really thought that far into the future.

He must have seen the look of dismay on my face, for he quickly added with a laugh, "Funny, but I think I have already grown used to it. Indeed, I suppose I suspected it all along."

I breathed a sigh of relief.

"But I hope you do not start correcting my vulgus on a regular basis, for I fear that having a love who considered herself my constant teacher might be a little too hard to take."

"I would never—"

"I am teasing, Bet. I am only teasing."

In fact, we had both had a lot to get used to since the night of my revelation, when I had informed James that I was Bet, had never been Will.

That first kiss, after he finally knew who I was . . .

❦

His lips pressed against mine, the exquisite and almost unbearable sweetness and power of it, the wonder . . .

It was almost too much, feeling his arms tighten around me, the imprint of his hands through the impossible thinness of that white nightshirt.

I think now that if things had progressed between us in the normal way, if there even was such a thing as *normal* in this world, we would have felt driven, unable to prevent ourselves from pressing further in this new physical journey. As it was, and as I say, even just that one kiss was almost too much.

Not to mention, I was still not willing to give up my dream of getting a proper education. But now, where before there had been only two people in the world who knew of my dream, Will and myself—unless one counted Mrs. Smithers and Mrs. Hunter, which, for some reason, I did not—there was a third who had entered the picture: James. And so stories needed to be told, explanations needed to be given.

But before even wanting to know how this had all come to pass, my presence at the Betterman Academy, James wanted to know why I had chosen to reveal myself to him in that moment.

It was a lot to admit out loud, and I could just barely be brave enough with his forehead pressed to mine, his strong yet elegant hands cradling the sides of my face.

"Because," I admitted, "you, and my feelings for you, have become more important to me than my original plan."

I pulled away a bit, looked up in time to see a slight smile spreading over his lips.

"And that plan was . . . ?" he prompted.

And so I had told him. I told him everything.

He was silent for a long time, as though it was taking his mind a while to understand the words his ears had just heard.

"Although you have had the advantage of knowing what it is like to be the opposite sex," he finally said, "*a boy,* I have never had the similar advantage of knowing what it is to be a girl. Still, I can well imagine now, based on what you have said, that there are frustrations inherent in your gender—"

He stopped and laughed. I had the sense that the laugh was at neither me nor our situation but at himself.

"No," he said, "that is all far too formal. I suppose that what I should say, more simply, is that sometimes it must be just downright awful being a girl."

For answer, I stretched up on my toes, touched my lips briefly to his again. "It does have some advantages," I allowed.

"Yes," he agreed, taking a deep steadying breath, as though he were trying to contain something within himself. "I will grant you that. If you were still Will Gardener, I would not feel so free to . . ."

He touched his lips to mine again, with more force than I had done. I did not mind it.

Pulling away, he asked, looking suddenly wounded, "Was there not a moment before tonight when you felt you could trust me with your secret? Was I not a good enough friend to you?"

Seeing his hurt, *I* felt hurt at having caused it. But I had to answer honestly.

"Yes, you were," I said, "but no, there was never such a moment before."

"I don't understand."

"It is not a matter of trust, don't trust," I sought to explain. "I always simply assumed that the truth was a burden that I alone must carry."

"But now you have halved that burden by sharing it with me."

"Yes. Yes, I have."

"And the real Will Gardener, of course, he always knew."

At first I thought I was hearing jealousy in the way he said this.

But no, I decided upon reflection. It was merely a slow acceptance of this strange new world he had wandered into.

And that was perhaps the most amazing thing of all to me: that he accepted everything, my strange story and the implicit lies I had been telling him all these past months, without rancor or blame.

"Yes, Will always knew."

"And he has had his own secret life all this time too." Concern altered his expression. "He has gone off to war, and you have not received a letter from him in quite some time."

"No." I heaved a sigh. "No, I have not."

Where was Will?

Following the night of my revelation, things changed dramatically between James and me, as one might imagine; some of those changes were sudden, while others were more gradual.

Before, I had not been willing to disrobe in front of James before bed for fear of exposing myself as a girl. Now, I insisted on closing the shutters so he would not see me naked because he *knew* I was a girl. It would have been too immodest, too much temptation. Still, once I exchanged my daytime disguise for my nighttime reality, I would stretch out with him on his bed, where we would hold each other and talk and kiss, sometimes a little more. Some nights, it was all I could do to tear myself away and return to my own bed lest we go too far. It was such a temptation, but one I could not allow myself. After all, I knew what had befallen my own young mother, having a baby out of wedlock—me—which had nearly resulted in her being put out on the street. Not to mention, if it was hard to hide being a girl at school, it would be that much harder to hide being a *pregnant* girl. As for James, that amazing boy, he seemed to accept the current limitations on our physical relationship without explanation. Indeed, some nights it was *he* who had to tell *me* when it was time for me to go back to my own bed!

"Really, Bet, I think it is time you—"

"But couldn't we just . . . ?"

"No!"

Let me just say that it was not easy, not for either of us.

In addition to the change in our bedtime rituals, there were other changes to get used to: the sheer joy we each felt upon waking to look across the room and see the other still there; the giddy feeling of liberation when, following dinner and after having returned to the room as James and Will, we would lock the door behind us and safely transform into James and Bet.

Then, too, there was James's newfound protectiveness of me.

When he sought to defend me against Mercy at dinner—Hamish had, of late, become peculiarly and uncharacteristically silent at mealtimes and even on the playing fields—I would try to tell him that he was being silly, but James would counter that *I* was the one who was being silly.

"You cannot very well expect me to sit idly by, Bet," he would say once we were back in our room, "and let others cast aspersions on the honor of the girl I love."

The girl I love—I had to admit, I liked that.

We had first confessed our love for each other on the night of my revelation. In some ways it had felt sudden, as though we had barely been properly introduced. And yet, somehow, it would have felt dishonest had we not done so, and there had been too much dishonesty between us already, at least on my part. Since that night, we had spoken those words, or words like them, regularly, daily even, and I never grew tired of hearing or saying them, never felt anything but wonder at the glory of it all.

"I appreciate that, James," I said now, "I really do. And of course it pains me too on those rare occasions when Mercy or Stephens dares to say something rude to you. But I have always fended for myself just fine here, or at least, I haven't gotten myself exposed or killed. If you start leaping to my defense every time someone does something as benign as lob a dinner roll at my head, surely the others will suspect something is amiss."

"But it is such a pretty head," he said, laying a kiss on the object of our discussion.

"That may well be," I said, "and I am forever grateful that you think so. But I do not want the others to think me weak or, worse, *feminine.*" I sneered as I spat out the word. "I do not want them to think of me as some sort of *girl.*"

At this, James threw back his head and roared.

"No," he said, once he had his laughter under control, "we certainly don't want that. Besides," he added, kissing my mouth this time, "I am finding that I rather like being the only one who knows that particular thing about you, the one who knows you better than anyone else."

Still, though I was unwilling to let James go out of his way to protect me, he was insistent that I do more to protect myself.

"What do you mean?" I demanded one night when he had informed me that my impersonation of a boy was slipping. "I have been doing just fine these last six months. *You* certainly never guessed the truth. Why, I had to practically disrobe in front of you in order to convince you!"

"Actually, Bet, you *did* disrobe in front of me, but you kept your back to me at the time—one of my few regrets in life. But no, I don't think your impersonation has ever been as good as you think it is, and lately, it has gotten worse."

I narrowed my eyes at him. "How do you mean?"

Not waiting for an answer, I grabbed a paper upon which I'd been writing a letter from Will to the old man back at Grangefield Hall. "Don't my letters look like a boy makes them?" Casting the paper aside, I strode back and forth along the short length of our room, the first time with great purpose, the second time casually and with hands in pockets as though idly counting my imaginary change. "Don't I walk like a boy?"

"Yes." He shrugged. "Or enough. But being a boy is more than poor penmanship and walking."

I barked a short and, I thought, masculine laugh. "Not by much."

"Oh, no. It really is."

I put my hands on my hips, feeling it a rather mannish stance. "Like what, exactly?"

"Like, well, drinking and smoking. I remember your first day here, as we were walking back from dinner, you claimed that both were frequent activities of yours—which, I must say, did strike me as a false claim at the time—and yet I've never seen you do either."

"Well," I said with a huff, feeling rather put out at this, "nor have I seen you do those things. Let me see . . ." I tapped a finger to my lower lip, cast my eyes toward the ceiling. "Have I ever seen you puff away like a chimney? Hmm . . . *no.* Have I ever seen you come into our room and fall down drunk? Hmm . . . *no.*" I dropped my tapping finger and returned my gaze to him. "See? There you have it. *You* don't do those things either."

"Well, but that's me," he said. "Everyone knows *I'm* odd."

I had to laugh at this.

"You also don't make fun of the other boys as everyone else does," he went on.

"Nor do you," I countered.

"You never get in fights."

"Not true. Don't you remember me fencing Hamish into the wall?"

"Yes," he conceded ruefully. "I had forgotten that one. Be that as it may . . ."

In the end, James wore me down. He convinced me that in order to continue my masquerade successfully through the remainder of the school year, which did not end until early July, I needed to become more *boy* than the boy I had been thus far.

"I can't say this is the best idea you've ever had." I hiccupped in James's general direction. *Demon beer,* I thought.

It was the following Saturday night; we'd already suffered through the weekly singing in front of the fireplace in the great hall, and now we were all freezing in the woods behind the playing fields, nipping away at the beer bottles Mercy had so thoughtfully provided. I'd smoked more, thanks to James's prompting, than I ever wanted to smoke in my entire life, and my throat was feeling raspy. Honestly, it was a good thing the cold evening air was so bracing; otherwise I was sure I'd have vomited all over the boots that Mrs. Smithers always kept so beautifully shined for me.

Ah, Mrs. Smithers, I thought fondly in my admittedly pixilated state.

"Such a pleasure to have you two with us for a change," Mercy said with what struck me as a forced geniality.

Hamish merely scowled.

Stephens merely scowled too. I'd gotten the sense that Stephens somehow blamed me for Hamish attacking him over dinner that night. Perhaps because his taunting of Hamish had been about my "sister"?

"Here, have another," Mercy said, replacing my empty bottle with a full one.

James tried to take it from me, but I grabbed it tighter and looked up at James beside me. He reminded me so much of Will then, in personality if not in looks, and the beer I was drinking reminded me of the way Will had encouraged me to drink at the pub that night on my first journey to Betterman. *Ah, Will.* But then I thought how different the two were, really. Yes, they were both boys; yes, they were both handsome; yes, they both wanted the best for me, in ways that no one else on earth did. But I'd never wanted to kiss Will the way I wanted to kiss James right then . . .

"My, it is cold out here tonight," James said, rising abruptly and moving away from me. Later on, I would realize what a kindness he had done me, for if he'd stayed right there next to me, in my drunken state I would have kissed him in front of God and everybody, as the saying goes. As it happened, I teetered and fell face forward into the cold dirt.

Poor Mrs. Smithers. She was going to have a devil of a time cleaning the dirt stains out of all our trousers. Didn't these boys ever drink indoors?

I pushed myself up to a sitting position. I was freezing.

"It is cold, isn't it?" Mercy allowed cheerfully.

I realized then that I must have spoken my thoughts aloud. I would have to watch that, I cautioned myself. *Demon beer.*

"And it would be a nice night," Mercy went on, "to have some female companionship to keep a boy warm, wouldn't it?"

"Too bad there aren't any around," James said. But as he spoke, I saw him spare me a smile.

Ah, James.

"Now, if Gardener's *sister* was here," Mercy said. "You remember—*his twin?* Now, there's a girl that could keep a boy right warm enough, I'd wager."

James's anger was instant. "Lay off Gardener's sister," he said, moving to stand in front of Mercy in a challenging position.

I was dimly amazed he could move so fast, given how much we'd all had to drink. Perhaps he'd drunk more in his life than I had? But I also felt a lazy smile touch my lips: James was standing up for me.

"Yesh," I slurred, stumbling to my feet to join James, "lay off my shishter."

I looked up at Mercy. Oddly, he didn't look as though he felt threatened by the situation he'd gotten himself in.

"You really are an odd one, Gardener, aren't you," he said, as if it were a new observation.

"Well, you know." I hiccupped. "I suppose I have my moments when I might appear *different.*"

"The night of the dance," Mercy said consideringly. "That illness came on you so suddenly. If one didn't know better, one would think you were scared of being around girls."

"Scared of girls?" I hiccupped again. "That's rich. I'm just what you might call *particular* about who I spend time, er, getting warmed up by."

"Oh?" Mercy raised his eyebrows. "And what sort of girls *do* appeal to you?"

Suddenly I remembered what James had said in an earlier discussion. In addition to pointing out that I was not like the others because I did not smoke or drink or regularly get into fights, he'd also said I didn't insult the others enough. Well, I was ready now.

"Well, I'll tell you one thing," I said, my own words striking me as incredibly funny. "If I ever wanted to get warmed up by a girl, it would never be one of *Hamish's* sisters."

And then I really did vomit.

❦

"Well, that went well," James said a half-hour later as he helped me get ready for bed.

"Do you really think so?" I mulled this over as he pulled my nightshirt over my head. "Yes," I answered for him, "I think so."

"The look on Hamish's face." He chuckled.

"Too bad I never saw it." I yawned. "Too busy vomiting."

Gently, James lowered me down onto my bed and stretched me out.

"I did all right, though, didn't I?" I asked, half sitting again. "I did well at being a boy?"

"Let's see..." He considered. "You got drunk. You smoked until it hurt. You got belligerent. Why, yes. I'd say you did perfectly."

I smiled. Then I draped my arms around his neck and attempted to pull him toward me.

"Would you like to kiss me?" I asked saucily.

James waved a hand in front of his nose. Oh, right. I hadn't done anything about my teeth yet. "Not tonight, I'm afraid. But I do love you, Bet."

Then he eased me under the sheets and tucked the crisp linen under my chin.

"I love you too, James." I sighed a happy sigh.

"Night."

"Night."

The next day, despite my pounding head, we laughed. We laughed a lot.

And so we continued, in our stumblingly awkward and yet blissful way, for a week, then another, and another, until spring came and with it the budding trees of late March and the end of Lent half. Soon we would break as we had for the Christmas holidays, this time until the end of April, at which point we would reconvene again for Summer half, which would last until early July.

It's amazing how long someone can hold a grudge, seething in silence, and how patiently a person can wait to eke out his revenge. Wait long enough, and the mark doesn't even see it coming.

They came for me in the night.

It was two hours after James and I had finished dinner at Marchand Hall. We were in our room, the door locked, which was a rarity at the Betterman Academy, when the jiggling started, followed by a loud pounding. Thank God, I thought, for that locked door, as James had just been kissing me. Thank God also that I still had on my day clothes, or at least my shirt and tie and trousers, for it would have been awkward to explain away the length of time it took for me to tear out of my nightshirt, bind my breasts with cloth, and get changed again before I answered the door. I laughed at the picture in my mind, stopped laughing when James unlocked the door and I saw Hamish standing there, fists clenched at his sides. Behind him I saw Mercy, Stephens, about a half a dozen others, and—was that Little in the back?

James faked an elaborate yawn. "Really, Hamish," he said, "it's just a few days till end of term. Isn't it a bit late in the season to be staging yet another tossing? And anyway, don't you ever get tired of that sort of thing?"

As it turned out, Hamish had another sort of tossing in mind, quite different from putting a boy in a blanket and throwing him in the air to make him squeal.

Hamish pushed his way into the room and commenced ripping the sheets off first my and then James's bed. He looked underneath the beds. He dumped the water out of our washbasins.

"Can we help you locate something?" James yawned again. "Preferably before you destroy the whole place?"

Hamish whirled on James. "I've never liked you, Tyler, you with all your . . . *smugness.*" He turned toward me. "And I like you *less.*"

Before James could respond, Hamish made for his wardrobe and threw wide the doors. He began tearing clothes out and tossing them at the other boys, throwing the things that displeased him right out the window.

"The sleeves on that shirt may be too long for you," he said, addressing Mercy, "but you can't argue with the fabric."

"Are you stealing my clothes?" James was incredulous.

Hamish shrugged. "Borrowing," he said. "Why should you have all the best things? I would think you'd be generous enough to spread it around a bit."

"I wonder what Mr. Winter would think of all this?" I said in as threatening a voice as I could muster.

Hamish snorted. "Not bloody much, I shouldn't think."

I stood straighter. "Perhaps I shall go get him and find out, then."

Hamish snorted again. "Fat lot of good that'll do you."

My eyes narrowed. "How do you mean?"

"Mercy brought him a little present," Hamish said with a sneering smile. "Told him that all those bottles of beer were a gift from his parents for his having put up with us all these months. Made a similar delivery to Mrs. Smithers. Come to think of it, the last time we saw them, they were enjoying an end-of-term snort together."

"I doubt we'll be seeing them before morning," Mercy added, giving a half bow in modest acknowledgment of his own contribution to the evening.

Having exhausted James's wardrobe, Hamish turned to mine. As

Hamish reached for the handle, I threw myself at his back. I suppose I should have thought of fighting them earlier, but there were so many of them and only two of us. Now, however, I was desperate.

Mercy and Stephens seized my shoulders and peeled me off Hamish. They needn't have bothered, I realized. Hamish could have tossed me off with a single shrug.

"Hey, what's this?" Hamish said, finding the wardrobe locked. He jiggled the handle harder, grew frustrated. He ran his hand along the top of the wardrobe, producing only dust that Mrs. Smithers had been too short to reach, and grew more frustrated. "No one keeps their wardrobe locked here. First your door was locked, now this. What are you two hiding?"

"Shall I go and fetch an ax?" Stephens offered.

"The key." Little piped up for the first time. "Will always keeps a key in his pocket. I-I-I saw it drop out of there the day we went fishing." Little must have felt my horrified glare boring into the side of his head, for he turned to look at me with a sad, apologetic shrug. "I'm sorry, Will. But you know there's never any point in running or hiding. They always catch you in the end."

I struggled, but there was little I could do as the two boys held me firmly while Hamish rifled through my trouser pockets. At this point, James also tried throwing himself at Hamish's back, to no avail.

"A*ha!*" Hamish exulted, key in hand.

But his exultation turned to dismay as he flicked through my things, removed a shirt here, a pair of trousers there.

"Huh," he said. "I don't see what the big secret is. These are just clothes, and not even as fine as Tyler's. Oh, well." He shrugged, tossed a shirt to Stephens. "Maybe one of the younger boys would like this."

I breathed a sigh of relief as Hamish moved to close the doors, but that relief proved premature as Hamish caught sight of the trunk in the bottom of the wardrobe. "What's this?"

All I could do now was stand helplessly by as, with what seemed like excruciating slowness, Hamish dragged out the trunk and opened the lid.

"What's this?" he said again, now clearly puzzled as he pulled out my dress, my wig. Confusion quickly turned to anger, however, as Hamish put two and two together and came up with . . . what?

"There was never any sister at all, was there?" he accused darkly. "*That's* why you begged off sick the night of the dance. It was really *you!*" And then anger turned to horror. "And I asked you to *dance* with me? You danced with Tyler and Little, while masquerading as *a girl?*" He paused for the briefest of moments, dress and wig still in hand. "What kind of an abomination are you?"

His horror was my opportunity.

I ran.

In a million years, I would never have imagined that I could outrun a group of boys, but the events that had transpired, coupled with my abrupt bolting from the room, worked to my advantage. Still, I felt no better than a wily fox briefly outsmarting the hounds as I raced down the stairs of Proctor Hall, raced across the grounds of the Betterman Academy, the dogs nipping at my heels. When it felt as though I could run no farther, my legs screaming in agony, my heart pounding as though it would slam right through my chest, I took refuge in the one place I thought I might find it: the chapel.

It seems such an irrational thing to me now. Did I think I was a character in a Victor Hugo novel, crying "Sanctuary!" at attackers? Had I forgotten that the right of asylum, guaranteeing a fugitive protection from arrest in the safe haven of a church, had been abolished in England some two hundred years before? Whatever the case, it was where I chose to make my stand. And curiously, once inside, I felt calm permeate my entire being as I took in the great painted window soaring over the altar, the pulpit itself fashioned in oak, the high gallery and organ behind. Even when the others burst through the doors and Hamish backed me up against the altar, that sense of calm did not leave me.

Could I still get out of this? I wondered. Perhaps I could say it had all been an elaborate practical joke? Hamish would surely beat me for it, since he would see the joke as having been on him. Still, it would be worth the severe beating, if only I could—

"What kind of an abomination are you?" Hamish roared at me again. "You made a fool out of us!" His voice turned deadly. "You made a fool out of *me.*"

Slowly, he drew his arm back and clenched his fist.

Not wanting to watch the blow as it smashed into my face, I glanced over Hamish's shoulder and saw James straining to get to me, Mercy and Stephens holding his arms tight.

"Don't hurt her!" James's desperate voice rang out, echoing through the cavernous chapel. *"Leave her alone!"*

Hamish's fist stopped inches from my face as confusion set in. *"Her?"* Then, as though obeying some animal impulse, he grabbed at the collar of my shirt and, with a great downward pull, tore through white tie and white shirt, his eyes nearly popping at the sight of the winding cloth that bound my breasts.

"What . . . ?" he said dumbly, his face purpling in embarrassment. "Why . . . ?"

Not caring at that moment for my own tattered modesty, I faced them all.

"You take it for granted!" I roared, for once using my own voice, that of a girl. "All of *this.*" I waved my arms at the chapel, at the very earth of the Betterman Academy that surrounded us; really, I was thinking of the whole world—a world that belonged to boys like them, never to the likes of me. "Don't you see? I wanted what *you* have." I spat out the last words: "What you hold so *cheaply.*"

The energy had left me, the fight was gone. It was all over now, I realized, all my fantastical dreams. Whatever I had once hoped to accomplish—finished.

James, free from Mercy and Stephens, made his way to me. Gently holding together the remains of my shirt in one of his hands so that the winding cloth was covered again, he put his other arm around my shoulders and walked me out.

CHAPTER *twelve*

It was a long way home.

And over the course of that long road home, during the carriage ride, no longer entranced by the novelty of cows—I had seen cows before—I thought back over what had transpired after James and I had left the chapel.

Seconds after we had closed the door to our room and I had done up the buttons on my white shirt, there was a loud knock at that same door. Without even waiting for an answer, Dr. Hunter entered the room. He looked as though he'd been roused from sleep; his black robe had been hastily thrown on, and he hadn't even taken the time to don his usual cap over his now wild hair.

"Gardener," he said, addressing me accusingly, "if that is even your real last name, you are to come with me."

Apparently the others, Hamish and the rest, had wasted no time in going to the headmaster with their tale. Funny, I thought distantly, feeling removed from the situation, Dr. Hunter hadn't wanted to listen to tales of others' mischief when I had been the person telling them.

He stood with his back against the open door, hand on the knob, imperiously, waiting for me to walk past him, and when I did, he pulled the door shut behind us, closing it on James.

We walked down the long corridor and staircase. Both were lined with boys who no doubt would have jeered me were it not for the sternness of Dr. Hunter's stride. I did catch one glimpse of Little. He mouthed the word *sorry.*

Outside, as we strode across the commons to his house, Dr. Hunter spoke not a word to me; the only sound was that of the wind beating his black robe, as though he were a great bird soaring through the night.

The interior of the headmaster's residence was as I remembered it, that odd juxtaposition of severity and comfort. As though to echo that, Mrs. Hunter was waiting in the room her husband led me to. She too looked as though she'd dressed hastily, throwing a luxurious dressing gown over her nightdress. But whereas her husband looked as though he were still laboring under a great shock, she did not look surprised at all, only sad, as though she had been half expecting this moment all along.

"I have made tea," she said with a gentle smile, waving her hand at the tray that sat on a low table.

Dr. Hunter accepted a cup.

"Leave us, my dear," he said to his wife.

She straightened her spine. "I prefer to stay."

He considered this for a moment. "Very well," he at last allowed. Then he turned to me. "Sit."

"I prefer to stand, sir," I said, not even bothering to sound like a boy, "if that is all the same to you."

He considered this too. "Very well," he allowed again.

And so all three of us remained standing.

"Now, I should like you to tell me how this all came about . . ." He paused. "I don't even know what to call you, miss. *Is* there even a Will Gardener?"

"Oh, yes," I said. "There is a Will Gardener and he is very much alive. Or at least, I hope that is still the case."

"Still the case? Did you . . . *do* something to him?"

I pictured what must be going through his mind: an image of me, a mere girl, somehow overpowering or even killing a boy so that I might assume his place.

"Oh no," I hastened to say, "nothing like that, sir."

"Then *what?*"

So I told him. With no other choices left to me, I told him everything.

"I have n-never," he stammered, "in all my years . . ."

"Is it not wonderful, my dear?" Mrs. Hunter asked him, a light shining in her eyes.

"Wonderful?"

"To think," she said, "of a girl wanting an education so badly she would go to such extraordinary lengths."

"How absurd!" Then he paused, reflected. "Huh." Dr. Hunter regarded me as though with new eyes. "I had not thought of it like that."

"But now that you *are* thinking of it like that," Mrs. Hunter pressed, "is there not something that can be done?"

His eyes narrowed now. "Done?"

I watched the match between them, unwilling or unable to interrupt the flow. It had been years since I'd had a mother to stand up for me, so long ago I barely remembered her, and yet I felt in a strange way as though I had one now.

"Yes, *done!* Year after year, so many boys pass through that front gate, not caring if they are here or not, regarding this place merely as a steppingstone to something greater or, worse, as an ordeal simply to be borne. But now you have someone that actually *wants* to be here. Someone who represents everything we desire our students to be."

I saw him bristle at her use of *our.* Still: "Yes," he said slowly, "I suppose one could look at it like that."

"Then how can you even think about casting Bet out?"

"Bet?" He looked at me, at her. "How do you know her name? She has not told us."

Mrs. Hunter waved a dismissive hand. Apparently she intended to explain all such trivialities later. "That does not matter now."

"Very well. Just what are you proposing?"

"You yourself have said that the person known as Will Gardener is the first in his—in *her* class." Mrs. Hunter shrugged her pretty shoulders. "Why can't she simply stay?"

Yes! I thought. *Why can't I?*

Then I saw the look on Dr. Hunter's face. He had never struck me as the sort of man who'd hit his own wife—indeed, despite what Mr. Winter had said to me once, I'd never heard any reports of Dr. Hunter even hitting the boys—but as a dark cloud rolled across his face now, he certainly looked sorely tempted.

"Because she can't." With great deliberation, he set down his teacup on the table. "Don't you both realize the impropriety of it all, the awkward position we have already been placed in? Why, she has been living in a room with that boy for—" He turned to me. "How long has Tyler known the truth about you?"

"He only just learned tonight," I said evenly, "along with the others." Whatever happened this evening, I would not let James hang with me, even if it meant telling a lie. James was my friend. He was my love.

Dr. Hunter nodded curtly, as though at least this small thing pleased him. "That is good," he said. He turned to his wife. "Surely you must see that she can't go back there and live with a boy."

Her expression was open, as though the answer were obvious. "Then why can't she stay here, with us? Why can't she continue with her education until it is completed?"

He stood frozen for a long moment then, causing me to wonder: Could he actually be considering such a thing? Oh! To remain at school, where James was, to be able to continue my education, only this time as myself.

Dr. Hunter turned to me, and I waited expectantly for what he might say. But when he spoke, his expression had turned sad, almost regretful.

"I am sorry, Bet." He waved an impatient hand. "Or whatever you are called. But you must see, surely you must appreciate—I must confess that what you have accomplished while here has been nothing short of astounding. To finish first in your class! And the time you backed MacPherson into a corner while fencing—oh yes, I did hear about that." He laughed a small appreciative laugh before something caused him to sober instantly. "The way you bravely stood your ground before me on Warren's behalf. If things were different . . ." He shook his head sadly. "But no. Things are not different. Perhaps there will come a time when girls can be at school with boys as equals, but that time is not *this* time. Certainly, it is not today. I am sorry."

With a hand over her mouth, Mrs. Hunter turned away.

"You must see," Dr. Hunter said, "that to keep you here would be chaos. And so you must go at once."

Then he turned away as well.

I was not even allowed to say goodbye to James; I left without seeing him again.

Someone was dispatched to my room to fetch my things, another someone dispatched to fetch a carriage so that I might be removed from the grounds immediately. It was as though if I were permitted to stay one moment longer than absolutely necessary, my mere feminine presence would contaminate the others.

And now we were pulling up in front of Grangefield Hall, and I was leaping out of the carriage. Not even waiting for the driver to take down my trunk, I set out immediately to find the old man. I was still wearing my Will Gardener disguise, and I was hoping to break the news to him gently before the letter arrived from the Betterman Academy informing him that "Will Gardener" had been sent down yet again, this time for "having misrepresented *her*self as a boy."

I found him seated in front of the fireplace in the drawing room.

"Who's there?" he called out, hearing my tread in the doorway.

Feeling as though I were re-creating the scene of my departure for the Betterman Academy, I went to him, knelt at his feet.

"Uncle," I said, using my Will voice.

He squinted at my face. "My dear," he said, a smile of relief stretching his lips. "You have come back."

My dear? How strange. I had never in my life heard him address Will so. And why the relief that I had come back? After all, Will Gardener was supposed to return home on this approximate date, at the finish of Lent half.

I shook off the feeling that something was not quite right. There was a job to do here. I needed to reveal all to the old man, preferably without giving him a heart attack, before that wretched letter came.

"I have something to tell you, Uncle," I announced clearly, my voice sounding a little too loud in my own ears. I brought the volume down. "Something has happened."

"Oh no." He put his hand to his cheek. "You haven't been sent down from school again, have you?"

This was harder than I'd thought. Yes, Will Gardener had been sent down from school again, but not in the usual way. And once the old man learned the truth, that it was *I* who had been sent down while impersonating Will—never mind how scandalized he would be by that—that's when the real concern would set in. He would begin worrying about the boy who had gone off to war, worrying about what had happened to Will.

What *had* happened to Will?

Perhaps, I thought wildly, I should continue with my impersonation a little longer? Perhaps it would be a mercy, a kindness, for the old man to think that Will was still here, safe, even if once again disgraced? I could forge another letter from Bet's new employer, I thought, telling him that Bet had grown so indispensable, she would not be returning home anymore. This would make things a little easier on me—I would not need to be forever going back and forth in my disguises, back and forth between boy and girl. Surely, if given the choice, the old man would prefer to have Will forever, even if it meant giving up the girl?

"Uncle," I began again.

"I like it when you call me that," he said, a pleased smile on his face. "I have missed having you around the old place."

What was he talking about? Will always called him Uncle, save for those times he called him sir.

Before I could say anything else, the old man leaned forward, placed a gnarled hand on my shoulder, drew me close enough to look me in the eye.

"You needn't pretend with me any longer," he said. "I *know,* and I am just relieved that you are finally back, safe, where you belong."

Know what? What *was* he talking about? Had his advancing years finally caused him to take leave of his senses?

I saw him cock his ear as though listening for something, and a moment later I heard it too. It was the sound of footsteps approaching from the hallway; the tread was slow and odd, with a peculiar tapping noise punctuating every second step.

I turned to see Will filling the doorway.

"Will!" I cried.

Not stopping to think, I rose to my feet, flew across the space that separated us, and threw myself into his outstretched arms, nearly knocking him to the ground.

It was only after we'd stood like that for a long moment, and Will had begun tapping my back as though he were starting to have trouble breathing, that I finally let him go.

And it was only then, for the first time, I noticed the cane in his hand.

"Will, what happened?"

"I was shot in the leg," he said, wincing as though the memory still pained him. Then he forced a manly smile onto his face. "Did you know that it can be just as dangerous in war to be the drummer boy as it is to be one of the men actually using weapons?"

He must have seen the look of horror that crossed my face—Will had been wounded! He might have been killed!—for he reached out his free hand, the one not holding the cane, and rested it on my shoulder.

"Please don't worry, Bet," he said gently. "I have survived it."

Yes, I thought, *yes, no matter what happened, he has survived,* feeling the relief wash through me.

We would get beyond this. I would help him in any way I could, without injuring his pride, of course. And before long, it would be as though the better part of the past year had never even happened.

But then the feeling of horror returned. What had Will and I just done? We'd been talking within the old man's hearing as though he weren't even there. Having heard Will talk about getting shot, he must surely realize that something was not right. Still, I thought, there *must* be a way to keep the truth from coming out. Perhaps we could—

"It is all right, Bet," Will said, his voice still gentle. Again, it was as though he'd been reading my mind, my concerns. Who was this new Will who suddenly possessed great power of empathy, the sensitivity to appreciate what others were feeling? Before I could marvel further at the changes in him, the way even his face looked years older now, he added, "Uncle already knows."

He took my hand, tucked it in the crook of his elbow, and started leading me toward the old man, his cane making it slow going.

What? I raised my eyebrows in startled question at him as we walked.

"He knows everything," Will said.

How?

"After I recovered enough to be sent home from the military," Will said, "I had to tell him the truth. It was still midterm, and although I suppose I could have lied and told him I'd been sent down yet again, that would have given me no proper explanation for this." Ruefully, he tapped his cane. "Much as Uncle never approved of my propensity for mischief, if he thought I'd been lamed at school, he'd have been up there like a light, demanding that justice be done. Wouldn't you, Uncle?"

We were right in front of the old man now.

The old man chuckled at the picture Will had drawn of him as a raging fury. "Indeed, I would have."

"But wait a second," I said. Then I narrowed my eyes at Will accusingly. "How long have you been home? And why did you not write to tell me what had happened?"

"I couldn't, Bet. Don't you see? If I had, you'd have rushed right back here to tend to me. You'd have left your own dream behind."

He was right. Had I known Will was injured, I would have done that.

"But—" I was confused now. I turned to the old man. "Once you knew that Will had been off at war and that I was impersonating him at school, why did you not send for me?"

"Believe me," the old man said, "I wanted to do just that. I was very worried. But Will begged me not to."

"He did?"

"Yes. Much as he would have liked to see you—his first weeks home were very hard—and much as I would have liked to see you, Will impressed upon me the importance of allowing others to fulfill their dreams. He said that it's only when people don't follow their dreams openly, in the way that they should be able to, that bad things happen, like drummer boys getting shot."

We all thought about that.

"So," Will said at last, mischief in his eyes, "*were* you sent down from school?"

"Oh, yes," I said calmly.

"For what, pray tell?" the old man demanded.

"This time," I said, "adding to his list of previous crimes, Will Gardener was sent down from school for impersonating a boy."

The old man threw back his head and roared.

❦

I changed into a dress, donned my wig once more, and we had supper. Over the course of the long meal, we laughed much, the three of us happy to be reunited once again, and I related some of the tamer exploits from my time at school. I ate more than my fair share, ate like a boy really, the sight of the glorious food making me realize how starved I was for it after the meager fare and mysterious meats of the Betterman Academy.

Then, stuffed and satisfied, we retired to the drawing room.

"Would you like me to read to you, sir?" I offered.

"Why, yes, dear, I do believe that would be—"

"Uncle," Will interrupted, "don't you think you should—"

"Yes," the old man said, "I really do think a bit of Shakespeare would be—"

"Uncle." Will spoke the word in a warning tone of voice.

"Very well," the old man said, coloring slightly. "I suppose it is time. But mightn't we wait until—"

"Tell her now, Uncle."

"Tell me what?"

"It's just that," the old man began, then stopped. "That is to say, once upon a time . . ." He paused again. "I suppose you have often wondered, dear, who your father was."

Funny, I *had* once wondered about that, but I hadn't given it a thought in a very long time.

"I have not," I said, "certainly not recently. I always assumed no one knew, or at the very least, that there was no one left alive who could tell me."

"Yes, well . . ." Still, he hesitated.

"Uncle."

"Fine!" the old man burst out. "Your father is the same as Will's!"

"The same as . . ."

"My nephew, Frederick. He was your father too."

"The same as . . ."

"I have no idea if Will's mother knew of this, but I can only assume that the identity of your father was one of the reasons your mother was not put out when she found herself in, er, the family way."

It was so much to take in. Surprise, wonder—Will really was my brother, then? Or at least my half brother?

Then anger set in, resentment.

"How long have you known about this?" I demanded of the old man.

Previously, he had spoken with a certain defensiveness. But now when he opened his mouth, the words that came out were tinged with a bittersweet quality.

"Since the first day I set eyes on you, my dear."

"Since the first day?"

"You were the spitting image of Frederick at that age, even more so than Will. I honestly couldn't understand how others didn't notice immediately, and yet no one else ever so much as commented on it. Perhaps people do not see what they do not wish to see."

I swung on Will. "And how long have you known?"

He held his hands up in front of him, as though I might physically attack him.

"Not long," he said. "After I returned home, Uncle told me. I suppose that once my own secrets were revealed, he felt guilty about the whopper he'd been harboring all these years. I must say," he went on, "after what I'd been through, it was the most wonderful of surprises, finding out that you really were my sister."

I remembered then what the old man used to say: there were no accidents in life, everything happened for a reason, everything happened out of choice or through design. And so it turned out that Will and I growing up together, looking so much alike, had not been accidental, had not been haphazard. Rather, it had all been part of the same fabric, even if we had not seen it from the start.

But there was so much I still didn't understand.

"But why are you only just telling me this now, when you have known for over a decade?" I said to the old man.

"Don't you see?" he said, sounding like a child hoping for forgiveness. "I couldn't tell you from the start. With Will's mother gone—what would her family have said? Do you think her family would have let me keep Will under those circumstances, never mind both of you? Of course not! They, and the larger world, would never have allowed that. A stink would have been raised. They would have kept Will themselves. And you, my dear—you they would have sent to the workhouse. Don't you see? I couldn't allow that."

"So you raised me here, somewhere between family and servant." It was so hard to let go of my resentment.

"I did my best. I did what I thought was best."

"But once I was here, why did you not tell me?"

"I wanted to. I wanted to tell you both. But in the beginning, I still worried that if the truth came out, you might be taken away. And as the years wore on . . . What can I say, my dear? I am an old man."

He was *so* old—I saw that now. Indeed, I doubted he was long for this world.

I went to him then, knelt at his feet, placed my hand on his arm. "Uncle," I said.

Will and I were out in the back garden, the master of the house having long since retired to sleep. We were seated on the curved bench, Will's injured leg straight out in front of him; he said it was now often stiff, and he could no longer pace as he once did. I wondered how much pain it caused him.

"So tell me," I said, "aside from being injured, how was it, being in the military? Was it everything you dreamed it would be?"

"Hardly." He snorted, but there was little humor in it. "As a matter of fact, I'd just as soon not discuss it. Suffice it to say that it was not half so . . . *glorious* as I'd imagined it would be." He eyed me closely. "How about you with school—everything you dreamed?"

"Hardly." I snorted too. "I wonder if anything is ever what people dream that thing will be."

Then I thought about James, kissing James, and decided that just occasionally, the dream did match reality.

As though reading my mind, Will asked, "And what of that roommate you fell in love with—what happened there? I had not wanted to ask about it in front of Uncle, but now . . ."

So I told him. I told him everything, right up to the last time I saw James standing alone in our room as Dr. Hunter led me away.

"What will you do now?" Will asked when I was done.

"Do? Why, nothing. What is there to do? It is finished."

"Bet!" Will was shocked. "I've never known you to be such a defeatist in your life! Don't tell me that you, *you* of all people, do not have some sort of . . . *plan?*"

"What sort of plan could there be?" I was exasperated. "James, like you, is the son of wealthy people. As for me, I am what I always was: the maid's daughter, with no prospects for the future." I saw him open his mouth to protest, cut him off. "I know. You will say that now we share the same father, and we do, for which I am eternally grateful." I covered his hand with mine. "But I am still, and always will be, the maid's daughter."

"Don't you think having a fortune might help with that? You know, despite how quick people are to judge, the evidence of all the schools that took me on no matter what I had done before proves that a fortune does help with people's perception."

"I have no idea, but that is not—"

"Possible. Oh, but it is."

"What are you talking about, Will?"

"Uncle. *Our* Uncle. After telling me that you and I share the same father, he showed me a copy of his final will and testament. It is his intention that his estate be split evenly between us two."

"Split evenly . . . ?"

"He says it is only just and fair, and I completely agree. I'm sure he would have told you earlier, but I think it took enough out of him as it was, telling you the secret he'd been keeping all these years. As he says, he is old; he gets so tired now. No doubt he was planning to tell you in the morning."

I was stunned.

"Don't you see, Bet?" he said when I remained silent. "You can write to your . . . *James* now. You can tell him how everything has changed, how you will one day have a fortune of your own, how now you two can be together."

"No," I said.

"No?"

"Nothing has changed."

"How can you say—"

"Because it is not how I want things to be. What, I would suddenly be acceptable, despite the circumstances of my birth—circumstances I had no control over, I might add—because now there is money in the picture? No," I said again, "that is not how I want things to be."

"Oh, Bet. Haven't you learned by now that nothing is ever as perfect as we dream it will be?"

"Perhaps not," I agreed. "But some things should be." I drew a deep breath. "Still, I will write to James soon. I owe it to him, to thank him for all his kindnesses to me. After all, he risked much, keeping my secret and then facing off with me against the others when they were so angry they might have killed us."

We sat in companionable silence for a long time then, breathing in the cleanness of the spring night.

"Funny," I said, "it is as though we never left here." I touched my hand to my artificial hair. "If not for your leg and this wig, it would be as though nothing had ever happened at all."

"Your hair will grow back," Will said softly.

A week later, having decided it was time, I got out paper and pen, intending to write a thank-you letter to James.

April 10, 18—

Dear James,

How odd it is writing you a letter when I have grown so used to talking to you face to face. I hope there was not too much trouble for you after I left. I am simply writing to properly thank you for—

I was interrupted by one of the servants, Molly, bringing in the post. There were exactly two items: a letter from the Betterman Academy, addressed to the old man—we would no doubt laugh as we read that together—and one for me, the return address of which began *James Tyler.* With trembling fingers, I tore through the seal.

April 7, 18—

Dear Bet,

I am writing you at the first opportunity time has permitted. I hope that this finds you well. You were forced to leave so abruptly, we did not even get the chance to say goodbye.

So much has happened since I saw you last! So much I want to tell you about!

Directly after you left, Dr. Hunter sent for me. He told me you had said that your secret identity was as much of a surprise to me as it was to everyone else. Oh, Bet! How kind it was for you to tell a lie in order to save me! But don't you see? I could never let such a lie stand.

So I told him the truth, how I had known for quite some time that you were a girl. Well, of course he raged at that. The impropriety of it all! Just as he sent you away, he sent me away too, with a letter informing my father of what had transpired.

But my father did not react in the way Dr. Hunter had perhaps envisioned. Rather, he was quite pleased with the whole thing. I never told you, but the reason I was sent to the Betterman Academy in the first place was that my father believed I had been too coddled all my life. He wanted me to attend a school where boys would be rougher, where I would need to fight for my way among them. He wanted to make a man out of me, a better man.

"This is wonderful!" my father said upon finishing Dr. Hunter's letter informing him that I had been sent down. "You have flouted authority! You have broken the rules! And when caught? Rather than lying to get out of it when you might have done so, you have stood beside the person you committed your crime with, taking your fair share of the blame rather than letting a comrade—is *comrade* the right word when one is talking about a girl?—stand alone. Why, I think you may finally be ready for Eton, my boy!"

What can I say? Remember how I used to tell you that you were odd? Well, as you can plainly see from my father's eccentric reaction, I well know what odd really is!

But never mind stern Dr. Hunter and my peculiar father. What I wish to know is: When can I see you again? Now, I know what you will say: that it is impossible, that our different stations in life make such a continued . . . *alliance* impossible. But don't you see? My father would care nothing about your beginnings—

he would probably be *proud* of it! And as for me, it has never mattered a tinker's damn to me. All that has ever mattered to me is you.

So, what's that you're saying? You'll have to speak up louder so that I can hear you. When did you say that I might come to call?

Awaiting your—hopefully speedy!—reply,
James

I crumpled up the page of the letter I'd started to compose and with a cry of joy tossed it in the air. Then, taking up a fresh sheet, I resolved to start anew.